The Ranks of Death

Marie Rowan

Published in 2017 by
Moira Brown
Broughty Ferry
Dundee. DD5 2HZ
www.publishkindlebooks4u.co.uk

ISBN 978-1-5220-2301-2

Dedication:

To John and Lisa Rowan with deep affection.

Acknowledgement:

I am indebted once more to Alan Jack of Salen, Isle of Mull, for allowing me to use one of his hauntingly beautiful photographs for the cover of this book. All his help in this is very much appreciated.

Chapter 1

Duncan Mitchell frowned very slightly, the merest hint of his eyebrows meeting together, before turning his grey almost colourless eyes slowly from the scene before him.

"There's Lady Grant." Mitchell nodded as the girl beside him stated the obvious. "Pity about Sir Ian dying in the Royal Infirmary. I told you about that, didn't I, sir?" Maddy Pearson, standing shivering in the snow beside Duncan Mitchell, sniffed loudly and Mitchell's attention was drawn to Lady Grant's party. He had seen them alight from a hansom into the maelstrom of bodies milling aimlessly around in the broad street of Edinburgh's Grassmarket. He watched closely as the four women plus one military officer picked their way as best they could through the rutted ice and deepening snow, with Captain Brogan clearing the way for them, towards the Black Swan Inn that Mitchell and Maddy had just left. Mitchell could still feel the warmth emanating from the hotel door behind him into the bitter breeze. The snow continued to fall in puffballs and Mitchell was not surprised that some coaches had been delayed the previous day on the journey to the Capital from Peebles. The Borders were under snow and even by now, Peebles itself might be snowed in. He watched the little group disappear inside the Peebles stagecoach and wondered who the other two women were. Lady Grant he recognised and also her lady's maid, Eliza Cowan, a woman who seemed to have captured Mitchell's eternal fascination.

"Mrs Campbell." The girl at his side seemed to be developing the uncanny knack of reading his mind. "Valley House - she's the other woman." Maddy was Crosteegan Castle's skivvy and part-time employee of The Mitchell Detective Agency. Mitchell was Lord and Lady Askaig of Crosteegan Castle's highly acclaimed butler.

"And the girl?" he asked.

"Think she's a relative - maybe," said Maddy.

"Maybes are not good enough. You don't actually know who she is?"

"Exactly." Another lesson learned by the fledgling detective. Mitchell was a stickler for accuracy.

Captain Brogan approached Mitchell when all the ladies had settled themselves in the stagecoach.

"A word, Mr Mitchell, if I may," he said. Maddy took the hint and moved away out of earshot.

"Whatever I can do to help, Captain, I'll undertake that task gladly." said Mitchell.

"Lady Grant is most anxious to reach Eddleston." Brogan's anxiety was deeply etched on his face.

"Home and familiar surroundings are definitely a comfort at a time of bereavement, Captain Brogan," said Mitchell. He had been told by Maddy of Sir Ian Grant's death earlier that day when he had met her at the hospital. Being in Edinburgh on personal business for several days, he had been directed by Lady Askaig to escort the girl back to Eddleston as she was being discharged following a ankle operation.

"Roderick Grant, Sir Ian's son, was supposed to meet us here in Edinburgh but it seems he has been delayed. I will be travelling to Eddleston, Mr Mitchell, but I find that I must now accompany the hearse. But I need to have a trusted male to watch over the ladies' welfare while they are on the coach. The hearse will travel a short distance behind. Would you consent to look out for them on the journey?"

"Of course, Captain Brogan, but why will you not be in the coach?" asked Mitchell frowning.

"Lady Grant is most anxious that no harm should come to her deceased husband's body." Brogan did not have to elaborate and Mitchell found disgust and outrage rise in his throat. Sir Ian Grant was a much-liked retired soldier and Mitchell had served under him very briefly.

"You will be paid for your vigilance, Mr Mitchell."

"I require no payment, sir," said Mitchell insulted by the very thought that the idea had been proposed. But the officer shook his head.

"Lady Grant insists and there is no way anyone will be able to change her mind. She is a very strong-willed person. Perhaps a donation to your favourite charity or something of that nature from the proceeds of a football match between my regimental football team your own one would be acceptable all round. Gifts to the poor, a local dispensary?" Brogan suggested. Mitchell nodded.

"If that's what it takes to ease the lady's mind at this sad time, Captain Brogan, then so be it."

"You already know the ladies, I think, Mr Mitchell."

"Not the youngest one," said Mitchell.

"Miss Lucy Cowan. She's a relative of Miss Eliza Cowan and Mrs Campbell who was a Cowan before she married. The young lady is a niece of theirs, I believe."

"But why travel along with the hearse?" asked Mitchell curiously.

"There was a vague threat to harm the general's body. A message received, unsigned."

"May I see it?" Brogan nodded somewhat reluctantly.

"It was simply a Christmas card with the words 'Till we meet again' written on it." Brogan carefully removed a small envelope from his pocket-book, extracted the card, glanced at it briefly, then passed it over to Mitchell along with the envelope. It was beautiful, a simple Christmas scene in blue and white embossed with a gold border. Mitchell was puzzled. It was totally innocuous, he thought.

"The fact that it is unsigned hardly seems to me a reason for such caution, Captain Brogan. People are busy, forgetful at this time of year." Mitchell waited for an explanation watching the late general's former Aide de Camp closely.

"The general's coffin was viciously desecrated this morning."

Chapter 2

Mitchell watched as Joe Petherbridge expertly stowed the luggage onto his finest stagecoach. The snowflakes were now whirling crazily in the cold air, the noise in the crowded street deafening, people scrambling, slithering and occasionally falling as they tried to move about the almost white-out scene. Christmas Eve was looming and people were anxious to get home. The four sturdy greys were already harnessed and eager for a run out. Mitchell felt warm inside, the roast beef meal he had just eaten giving a glow which had been supplemented by the beaker of punch pressed upon him by the landlady of The Black Swan Inn. The light about them was fading although it was still only early afternoon, the darkening of the winter's day brought about by the heavy snow-clouds piling up above them. As the ladies were the only occupants of the coach apart from himself, Mitchell now shifted his attention to the iron rungs leading up to the seat beside Petherbridge and he finally decided to make his way up them. He closed the door of the stagecoach firmly. One glance told him that Captain Brogan and the hearse were waiting patiently behind.

"That's it, Joe!" But Petherbridge was hailing two latecomers across the width of the Grassmarket.

"On top, gentlemen!" he shouted through the noisy crowd before turning to Mitchell. "Another two fares are always welcome, Duncan," he said as the two men, muffled against the cold, handed their bags to the guard. Two? Mitchell looked at Petherbridge curiously. He had had the choice from hundreds milling about for the past few hours desperate to book passage on the coach. Still, he decided, maybe they were regulars and Joe was not keen to lose continuing custom by turning them away. Mitchell nodded and prepared to climb on top with the others. What had alerted him, he never knew, but he hesitated, foot poised on the iron rung and the sharp stone just caught him a heavy blow.

"Criminals!" Petherbridge shouted angrily. Blood spurted from Mitchell's head wound as he was pitched forward, his face taking the full force of the iron bar on his forehead as he went down as if pole-axed.

The deepening red that tinted the pristine whiteness of the newly-fallen snow told of the blood that was oozing from the wound, but in the darkening light of that winter's afternoon, it went unseen by Mitchell as he passed out, face down, into the depths of the bitterly cold snow. At some point, he was aware of being turned over, free now of the suffocating snow, but drifting in and out of consciousness. Voices came to him, clear and close by, and then muffled and distant and he knew he should rise, take control, but he couldn't. Mitchell's limbs were leaden, signals from his brain confusing the messages he was trying to send to them. Fegarty and Killilea had been killed. Get help. Tell the general. No, they weren't dead. He could hear their voices. Yes, they were dead. He'd helped bury their mangled remains, helped carve out the grave from the ice-bound ground at Inkerman. The Crimea was so cold. But he could hear their voices.

"Is it you, boys? Michael? Dominick? Is Dominick with you Michael?" Searing pain shot through Mitchell's entire body and then he suddenly felt the gentle, comforting softness of the nurse's hand smoothing the blood away from his eyes.

"Lie still" she whispered, "be at peace." He saw her face once more drifting before him then fade away to nothing. He felt the pain subside a little, the silence and void left by her begin to be filled with feeling and sounds. Voices came again.

"A head wound? Is it very serious?" Who was asking that? Mitchell wondered.

"Michael? Dominick?" he shouted again. Mitchell struggled up onto one arm, half-expecting to hear gunfire, agonising screams, to be minus a limb. The ice burned into him like fire and he passed a hand over his eyes.

"Are you alright, Duncan?" Joe Petherbridge's face swam into view, backed by the yellow glow of the Black Swan's lanterns. "Duncan!" Joe's voice was more anxious this time.

"I'm fine, Joe, just fine." Mitchell had to be in control. "What happened?"

"Somebody threw a snowball. Irresponsible swine! Nearly took your head off."

"Stone-filled?" Mitchell slurred the words and he hoped that that was the result of the snow numbing his mouth not a brain injury. Joe was speaking again.

"Worst part was when you pitched hard, head first, onto the iron rungs of the ladder. God knows how you survived that. Think anything's broken?"

"Probably not." Mitchell really had no idea.

"Well, you'd best be prepared for one hell of a lot of pain from those bones." And bruising, thought Mitchell. He lifted a handful of snow and gingerly placed it against his left cheek. What a spectacle he was going to make at Lord Askaig's Christmas entertaining.

"You were out cold for nearly ten minutes, Duncan. It put the fear of death into the ladies." And me too, Petherbridge could have added but didn't.

"Sorry about that." Ten minutes of hallucinating! Mitchell wondered if he had really been talking out loud. Hoped like hell he hadn't. The Battle of Inkerman was something he only relived in times of great stress and intense depression, both legacies of that conflict. He just had to know. "Hope you kept Maddy and the ladies inside the coach, Joe." Maddy had probably leapt to the rescue and was probably writing up her notes right then. Petherbridge smiled

"No curses, Duncan, not even one. Mrs Campbell beat Maddy Pearson to it and made her stay inside. She's a nurse of sorts - or was, it seems. She stayed beside you until you began to recover." Mitchell stood up shakily and leaned against the coach. "I think, Duncan, you'd be better off inside the coach. In the state you're in, I'll have to leave you behind if you don't for there's no way you're fit for sitting on top and not falling off." Mitchell closed his eyes and took a deep breath. He could hear the almost inaudible mutterings of the passengers on top. Everyone was anxious to be on the road to Eddleston, a few miles short of Peebles, and no-one more so that Mitchell himself. He tried to nod his agreement but the pain from even the slightest movement was intense.

"Fine by me," he agreed. "I'll sit inside. There should be room enough." Petherbridge opened the door and the ladies re-jigged their positions to accommodate Mitchell.

Mitchell leaned back and closed his eyes as his head was once more engulfed in pain. Excepting Maddy, he decided, what they had here on the stagecoach could be a reunion. A Crimean reunion. Crazy thought| Why had that thought entered his head? Their general, Sir Ian and Captain Brogan, his old ADC - but he had not been at Inkerman, travelling right behind them, Lady Grant and Miss Eliza Cowan who had waited nearby till the fog-blanketed battlefield of Inkerman ceased to be a hell-hole for the soldiers that day, and Margaret Campbell nee Cowan, who had nursed the dying and wounded including Mitchell himself. All of them were being guided through the snow right then by another old comrade, a marine from the Naval Brigade, from the same battle, Joe Petherbridge. And, of course, Mitchell himself. His's eyes opened slightly and his look met Margaret Cowan's for the first time in fifteen years. Her gaze faltered first and he wondered why she was travelling on the same coach as Michael Fegarty and Dominick Killilea, the two men now seated on top of the coach, two men Mitchell himself had helped bury at Inkerman just before the battle and who were now hell-bent on killing him for Mitchell had no doubt they had paid someone in the vicinity to cause his head injury. Had it merely been a warning of worse to come?

Chapter 3

Mitchell forced himself not to scream as the stagecoach began bumping its way over the icy ruts of the Edinburgh street. He succeeded, but only just. Pain exploded along a pathway through his head, his body stiffening as he fought to keep control. It subsided after what seemed like an eternity but he knew it had only been five or six seconds. Beads of sweat had broken out on his forehead and his surreptitious dab at them with his pristine white handkerchief was closely watched by Margaret Campbell. He avoided her eyes. The handkerchief was slipped discretely back into his travelling-cloak pocket.

"Looks like we're on our way, ladies." He was stating the obvious but his controlled tones reassured Maddy who was seated on his left. Lucy Cowan sat further along the seat on Maddy's left. Lady Grant gazed out of the window as she sat deep in her own thoughts opposite Lucy, Eliza Cowan between her and Mrs Campbell. The shadows were lengthening, the snow clouds ensuring darkness would come early on this cold, December day at the end of 1869. A sharp frost was inevitable, the air about them becoming increasingly bitter, the wind biting. It was intensely cold within the coach despite the small interior housing six adults in its compact space. Surely six bodies would provide some improvement in the temperature eventually, Mitchell hoped. Despite his travelling cloak, Mitchell's legs and feet were beginning to resemble blocks of ice. He closed his eyes as the pain in his head finally subsided to a thunderous throb.

"Try to sleep." Margaret Campbell could have been talking to any one of the women present but Mitchell instinctively knew she was not. He spoke as he slowly opened his eyes.

"I'm very grateful to you, Mrs Campbell, for your help, concern and excellent advice." Memories flooded back and the brain activity, such as it was, sent the pain soaring through him yet again.

"Then take it, Duncan." All life seemed suspended, her words soft and intimate. Maddy involuntarily sat a little more upright, a little more in suspense as she noted the use of her employer's first name. But Mitchell knew Margaret Campbell of old and her words and look held no surprises for him and if they did for the others, they should not have. Margaret Campbell knew Duncan Mitchell in every possible way that a good nurse should and both Lady Grant and Eliza Cowan were aware of it. Only Mitchell it seemed had been unaware that his nurse at the Battle of Inkerman fifteen years previously was in fact Eliza Cowan's sister. He had never known her name, only her touch, her face and her voice as he had fought death and, with her help, had finally won that battle. When had she first realised that Lord Askaig's butler was one of hundreds she'd nursed in that conflict? Why had she remembered him among the legions of soldiers passing through Scutari maimed, bloodied, scarred in mind and body, in rags and near starvation? She laughed softly, her fine features showing undisguised amusement as she almost openly went through his stages of puzzlement till the final solution came to him. The Highland Brigade! That was it. She had had a brother once in the 73rd, the other of the two Black Watch regiments and Mitchell had been a corporal in the 42nd. Killed in the early days of the war, Mitchell remembered, in the Crimea. She had always taken a particular interest in the welfare of The Black Watch soldiers. Thank God for that for it had been her perseverance that had saved his life. He felt she could read his every thought and decided to take refuge in feigned sleep. A head injury had caused him to relive an episode from the past, probably triggered by the face of a nurse last seen there in similar circumstances. But first Mitchell had to know more about the two latecomers. He was about to place an enormous amount of faith in Maddy's ability to be given one idea and run with it. He held out his hand and Maddy, understanding, passed the little notebook to him. He opened the notebook at the first page.

"If this is the new notebook in which you intend keeping hints and tips from the kitchen, Maddy, then you'd better put your name and occupation in it so that no-one else can lay claim to it. Like this. Name. M Pearson." He wrote it down. "Place - Crosteegan Castle, Eddleston, Peeblesshire.

Date. December 1869." He wrote that down too. "Finally, occupation, Skivvy." He also wrote 'Two strangers??' But only Maddy would know that. "There now, keep it safe and Cook will be most impressed. Now I shall sleep for a while." His eyes closed as he handed Maddy back her new notebook and silence fell within the coach, darkness already having crept upon them, only the blinding whiteness of vast expanses of snow bordering the narrow ribbon of road to be seen as Joe Petherbridge pushed on as far as it was humanly possible to go on their way into the Midlothian countryside and eventually the rolling hills of Peeblesshire.

Mitchell tried to relax. There was no telling how soon Petherbridge would be forced to stop. The deeper into the countryside, the more frequently were the huge snowdrifts beginning to appear. He was listening carefully but only the dull, quiet thud of Maddy habitually opening and closing her notebook punctuated, however slightly, the all-encompassing silence within that coach as the snow continued falling He heard Maddy cough softly before she began speaking.

"Miss Cowan, is there anything I could fetch for Her Ladyship and the other ladies at our first stop? Something to eat? A hot drink? Another rug perhaps for if it's only a short halt in West Linton and you might not all have time to get out? Mr Petherbridge might want to press on due to the weather instead of stopping for a hot meal." Duncan Mitchell relaxed for Madeleine Pearson was in her finest professional mode disguised as Maddy, the skivvy, always at everyone's beck and call. He wanted to glance at her, give her the nod of professional approval but resisted the

13

temptation for right then, he was Duncan Mitchell, Lord Askaig's butler and she was Madeleine Pearson, detective. He listened intently and somehow knew that Madeleine in full flight would be a joy to hear and a lesson to be learned. Maddy was his latest part-time recruit to the agency.

"I don't think so," said Eliza Cowan tersely. She spoke without turning her gaze away from the surrounding countryside despite the almost blinding whiteness of the snow. Eliza Cowan's voice could barely register any interest, her thoughts miles away.

"Yes, ma'am." There was a long pause and then Maddy's anxiety came to the fore yet again. "I can write very clearly, you know. I'll write down what you might want. Mincemeat pies, hot ones that is, that would help warm all of you up. Yes, that would help a lot." She began mumbling to herself as she wrote laboriously. "Mincemeat pies for four." Maddy, the skivvy, knew her place. "And something hot to drink," she added. "Now I wonder." She went off into more ramblings, soft and contentious they appeared to be, and her annoyance with herself for failing to reach a decision was obvious from her rapid scratching out of each successive idea she noted down. She shuffled her feet which Mitchell realised must be absolutely freezing. His own feet were clad in thick woollen stockings inside very sturdy boot and yet he was beginning to suffer pangs of cold in that region. God only knew how hers were feeling.

"It's the two gentlemen who came late. What am I to do?" Maddy was mumbling to herself again and the opening and closing of the notebook was becoming more rapid. "I'll have to jump out as soon as we stop. I'll just go ahead and ask them and then hurry into the inn. Mr Mitchell says the coach always stops for an hour or two at the Regent Moray Inn in West Linton. But that's not in weather like this. Maybe no-one will see me especially if it keeps on snowing. That would be the footman's work at Crosteegan Castle, fetching drinks and the like. I suppose Mr Petherbridge really will stop at the inn. Briefly probably. Oh dear! And what about Captain Brogan? I'll have to get something for him. Spiced ale. All the men at Crosteegan like that. Maybe I'll just do that. Order it for all of them and that way I don't actually have to speak to the two strangers. Lady Askaig certainly wouldn't approve of that. Then again, maybe it would look like I'm neglecting travellers and it almost Christmas Eve. They sounded foreign and being in a strange land at Christmas time must be very trying. Did they seem foreigners to you?" asked Maddy of no-one in particular.

"They're not foreign. They're Irish. They will be attending the general's funeral in Eddleston when it is arranged," said Mrs Campbell. Maddy seized on this reprieve.

"Well then, Mrs Campbell, ma'am, do you know then what they might want to drink?"

"What men all like. Ale, bread, cheese. Now let's just wait and see what happens. If we reach West Linton and stop for a reasonable amount of time, the problem will solve itself." So Mitchell had not been mistaken. He was convinced of that. Two Irishmen, Fegarty and Killelea. Though he were dead, yet shall he live, as the Bible said - times two. And they were here for Sir Ian's funeral. How did Margaret

15

Campbell know that? Had they spoken to her while he had been unconscious? There was not only something badly wrong with this, in fact everything was wrong with it. Where had they been all this time? Fifteen years! How had they managed to appear so soon after the death? It was no more than a matter of hours since Sir Ian had breathed his last.

"By the way, Miss Cowan," whispered Maddy, "I was so sorry to hear that Sir Ian had died this morning ."

"Sir Ian died three days ago," came the curt reply that silenced Maddy for good.

Chapter 4

Mitchell's mind was stunned. Three days dead! Why wait all this time to transport the body? And why had Petherbridge accepted two passengers at the last minute having refused time and again dozens of others who were stranded in The Grassmarket days before Christmas? Why those two or had he been waiting for them all along? Room only for the mourning party plus Mitchell and the unfortunate Maddy. Mitchell now had a growing feeling he had been right all along. He was in the middle of a revenge conspiracy and he had better find out fast who was involved and what he himself had done to get on the list of victims, assuming that he and the general's body were only part of it. A sudden jolt followed in quick succession by the coach skidding and skewing before up righting itself had him on full alert.

"Snowdrifts," he said to the ladies smiling ruefully and, hopefully, reassuringly. The long afternoon had moved into early evening and there was now no sign of the falling snow easing up completely. It was hard to make out landmarks and he could only guess that given the time, distance and the severity of the road conditions they had experienced for the past interminable hours that they were still some way short of a possible overnight stop at West Linton. But an early stop was perhaps just what was needed. He desperately wanted to speak to the two Irishmen, to reassure himself that resurrection was just a figment of some deluded religious fanatic's imagination. Fegarty and Killilea were dust somewhere in the frozen hills of Inkerman He also wanted more than a bit of polite chitchat with Nurse Margaret Campbell. But Joe Petherbridge might just be able to shed some light on it all for Mitchell felt sure Joe had been hired with specific passengers in mind. Was Mitchell himself on board because, no matter what, nobody refused a request from Crosteegan Castle or was he indeed part of the plot? The coach had come to a dead halt and Mitchell eased himself out into the icy depths some two feet deep in places. The road was partially blocked a few hundred yards ahead.

"Where the hell are we, Joe?" asked Mitchell well out of earshot of the women.

"A mile short of the Regent Moray in West Linton. But it might as well be a million," Petherbridge added sourly.

"Surely not. You've got the clearing equipment, Joe. There are enough able-bodied men here to clear that drift. We could shift it in no time. The road looks reasonably clear beyond it." Granted Mitchell could not see all that far but he felt Petherbridge was giving in too soon.

"Black ice, Duncan. That and the horses being dead beat is a recipe for disaster. The greys have been plunging through the drifts and if I were to urge them on for even another half-mile, they'd drop dead. I've got the best teams in the county and I mean to keep it that way. I was stopping nearby anyway to let the two Irishmen off." Petherbridge rubbed his eyes with his sleeve. "My eyes are nearly out of my head. All that whiteness nearly blinds a man. How's your own head, Duncan?"

"Shooting pains and a thumping headache. They're taking turns," said Mitchell wryly.

"Well, I'll soon have you out of this. It's not the Regent Moray but it runs it a close second."

"You've got me intrigued, Joe."

"Collinge Woods Priory. That's where the two men were to be dropped off. A slow trot along the road for a hundred yards, a right turn just before the snow-bank then up that elm-lined avenue, another turn off it and into the Priory drive. You'll be treated like latter-day saints by your old mate Brother Walter and the monks. Nice little guest-house, fine cooking by a brother who gave up austerity years ago and a guaranteed first-rate night's sleep in a clean bed." Mitchell smiled broadly and could not wait to rest his head on the promised fresh, cool pillow. Duncan Mitchell knew the Priory well. It was a favourite getaway of Lord Askaig's. The pain was beginning to slow down his thought processes and it seemed like an eternity since he'd last eaten properly. Mitchell readily gave in.

"I'm sure the ladies will be relieved to be out of this frozen waste, Joe, but what about Captain Brogan?" The hearse had long since vanished from sight. Both men looked back along the highway and through the now lightly falling snow.

"We'll wait here until they show up. I'd prefer not to leave my man out here to wait for him. It's too cold and we're both tired out. If he sits on a log and falls asleep, he'll never waken up. They have an old medieval charnel house at the Priory if Lady Grant doesn't want Sir Ian in the church. I don't remember the Grants being at all religious and people have definite ideas about that kind of thing." Mitchell grinned as Joe continued. "If I remember correctly, Sir Ian placed his faith in his men and their training in the Crimea."

"Joe, tell me this. Were you hired specially to transport the general's party back to Eddleston?"

"That I was," replied Petherbridge whilst doing his best to get the circulation moving again in his hands.

"How was it then that I wasn't transferred to the Swift Swallow? They often take your surplus business?" Mitchell dreaded the answer he knew was coming.

"You were on the list I was given. The girl's additional presence could be coped with." Mitchell's suspicious brain went into overdrive. But Joe Petherbridge's thoughts were now focused on other matters. "That monk at the Priory - the cook."

"Brother Conraitus," said Mitchell.

"That's the one. Well he's some cook and you will not be disappointed because not only is he probably preparing the fare of the quality that you're used to from His Lordship's occasional sojourns here, but also as it's Christmas soon, he'll be well into seasonal sweetmeats and the like as well. They usually expect stranded travellers when the weather is severe like today. I wish to god that hearse would hurry up. It was right behind us as we passed through Penicuik. Probably sliding all over the place. That'll hold them up. I don't envy Captain Brogan having to travel all this way beside a corpse."

"He's a soldier, Joe. He's used to death." Petherbridge nodded and rubbed his gloved hands vigorously to keep the blood flowing.

"He was like a son to Sir Ian. More so than his own was to him." Joe Petherbridge walked back to the coach to break the news about the overnight stay at the Priory. The two muffled strangers had descended and were standing on the far side of the coach, but too near it for Mitchell to tackle them right then. Petherbridge, having broken the news, slowly trudged back to rejoin Mitchell, still looking hopefully back along the darkened road for the hearse.

"Who are the two men, Joe? They're not from these parts."

"Irish by the sounds of it." He squinted at his passenger list in the harsh light of the rising moon, the snow storm now reduced to intermittent flurries. "Mr Michael Purcell and Mr Dominick Garry. Old comrades, do you think? The general's old regiment, maybe. It was an Irish one, I think."

"It was, Joe. The 88th. Galway. Great body of men." Petherbridge gave an almighty laugh.

"Yes but who could forget you and your mates, The Highland Brigade, swaggering its way along the streets of Plymouth in your red jackets and green kilts. A sight never to be forgotten."

"The good old days, Joe, when my knees were guaranteed to sweep any girl off her feet." He almost laughed at the absurdity of expecting two strangers with Irish accents to be called Fegarty and Killilea. But Michael and Dominick? He was also sure he had recognised the voices and Mitchell was not big on coincidences. "Maddy Pearson saw Lady Grant and her party at the Royal Infirmary of Edinburgh this morning while Maddy was waiting to be discharged. If the general died there three days ago, why were they there, Joe? Any idea?"

"Probably because the general's a general and if he needs a bit of space until he's ready to travel to his final resting place, he gets it. The likes of you and me breathe our last one minute and exit the back door on a handcart the next if that's all the undertaker's being paid for. No fuss, no ceremony. Down among the dead men post haste so that we don't spread disease. Adam Spanswick, whose hearse has been hired, collected the general's body from the hospital this morning with the family in attendance. He saw that the coffin had been desecrated. Shocking business but naturally he said nothing. That's what his driver told me back at The Black Swan Inn." So it followed that some sort of desecration had taken place in the hospital morgue. You had to be in possession of a truly sick mind to do that, thought Mitchell, and a shiver tore through his body.

"Head still giving trouble, Duncan?" Mitchell nodded and immediately regretted it. His mind had ceased to function clearly. He needed to rest. How could a simple blow to his head have such a lingering effect on him? He had a body scarred in more places than he cared to count.

"Mr Mitchell, sir!" He turned and watched as Maddy nimbly stepped out of the coach and her legs disappeared to mid-calf in the freezing snow. "Mr Mitchell," she repeated and began to fight her way through the snow bank by the side of the road, her stark form outlined by the intense brightness of moonlight and snow.

"Wait there!" he called. She had probably already undone the surgeon's best efforts at fixing her ankle by jumping down. "Wait there!" he repeated sternly and this time His Lordship's skivvy obeyed His Lordship's butler. "You, my girl, were supposed to stay in the coach," he chided Maddy gently.

"Here it comes! The hearse!" Joe Petherbridge pointed back along the icy depression that was all that marked out the highway from the surrounding snow-covered fields. The black carriage slowly covered the distance between them and halted, waiting to follow the stagecoach. Petherbridge left them and spoke quietly to Captain Brogan and the driver of their revised plans. Maddy hugged her notebook close to her chest.

"A word, please, sir." Maddy could hardly stop herself from shivering with cold, her lips almost numb, her hands bare and mottled red and blue. She saw him glance at her hands. "Must have dropped them in the snow back at the inn - the gloves."

"Say what you have to say, Maddy, and be quick about it." His voice was harsh and her eyes went down quickly to the ground. "Her Ladyship will have my head if you catch pneumonia while I have responsibility for you. Talk fast and get back in there. We're staying the night at Collinge Woods Priory not half-a-mile from here." Maddy could barely disguise her pleasure at this news. Something to drop casually in Crosteegan's kitchen when she returned and what an effect that would have among the other servants!

"It's about the two men, sir. They are Irish as you probably heard in the coach. I'm sure they know Mrs Campbell. Just a nod by one of them to her as well but it meant something more than just a polite gesture." Mitchell smiled at Maddy and promised himself that he would ask Mrs Brady, the Castle cook, and yet another part-time member of the Agency staff, to get the girl a proper rig-out for detecting.

"Well done, Maddy."

"All as before, the men outside, the ladies and Mr Mitchell inside," called Joe Petherbridge and then he prepared to ease his team of greys on again.

Chapter 5

Mitchell's head had begun to ache badly again. He wanted to get out, walk the remaining distance. In that weather? Was he going mad, too? One of the monks could rustle something up from the herb garden the Priory was famous for to give him a good night's sleep. A violent stabbing pain shot through his brain and he felt physically wiped out when it subsided. Margaret Campbell was watching him closely. He managed a smile he hoped was friendly and respectful but knew it was crass verging on the vacantly idiotic.

"Collinge Woods Priory has a fine reputation for hospitality, am I right, Mr Mitchell?" Lady Grant's dark eyes rested on him as she spoke for the first time and he forced himself to fight the weariness that was coursing through him.

"I can vouch for the veracity of that, Lady Grant. Lord Askaig has enjoyed several short stays here of a contemplative nature." Some hope. The Priory wine cellar always had to be completely restocked once his Lordship and friends left.

"And where Lord Askaig goes, so goeth his butler," she remarked.

"Quite so, my lady." For 'contemplative' read 'escape from the wife's relatives'. With a sudden jolt, the coach began the final lap of that long day's hazardous journey.

"Captain Brogan has now caught up with us I'm told, Mr Mitchell," said the widow.

"That he has, Lady Grant." A curt nod of the head and the ghost of a smile played about her lips. All was in order, her husband dead but safe. Silence descended within the moonlit coach, only Petherbridge's gentle urging of his horses breaking the silence of the countryside.

The wide avenue they turned into ran flat and straight and on beyond the main gates of the Priory. The medieval building stood some five hundred yards to the south. They turned off through the mighty gates wedged open by several feet of snow. The coach guard deftly rang a bell suspended from a sturdy post as they came through to warn the monks of their approach. The Priory's ruined transept disturbed the balance of a once beautiful structure, leaving a haunting melancholy in its place. The fitful midwinter moon increased the harshness of the ruins as their jagged fingers seemed to claw their way to some celestial peace. The windows, arched, tracery broken in part, stood silent and neglected, dark, lifeless and soul-less. The coach slid to a shaky halt and Mitchell's commune with dead souls passed.

"Welcome to Collinge Woods Priory," called a muffled voice as the heavy Priory door was firmly wrenched open and a hearty, yellow glow flooded the interior of the coach. "Lady Grant, our condolences, Mr Mitchell, welcome as always." Brother Walter's lamp banished the gloom and, behind him, the well-lit interior of the Priory cloisters beckoned Petherbridge's tired passengers. The road to the guest-house had skirted the old remains of a once-proud, soaring monastic church, leaving yesterday's sorrowing for the past and moving on through the centuries to the restored and welcoming buildings of the Priory precincts. The monks had wisely left the decayed victim to history and now seemed content with a monastery much-reduced in size but eminently more manageable. The new church itself seemed almost as great in size as the ruined medieval one. Mitchell nimbly alighted and was in time to see the hearse vanishing behind the ruins to the north and presumably on its way to the old charnel house near the still much-used infirmary. Wordlessly, he helped the ladies from the coach as Petherbridge and some of the monks quickly removed the luggage, Petherbridge's guard holding the tired horses. Maddy was already nipping Brother Walter's ear and even in the flickering glow of his lamp, the monk seemed relieved that someone would be taking responsibility for the ladies' needs in this all-male establishment.

"Are you inundated with stranded travellers, Brother?" Mitchell asked. Brother Walter shook his head.

"Only your party, Duncan. Father Prior had decreed yesterday no guests except those already booked in before today. We heard about Sir Ian's death and that his body was being taken back to Eddleston. We also realised that with the storm, the journey might have to be broken so we are not totally unprepared." Mitchell walked beside the tall monk along the well-lit cloisters bordering the south wall of the Priory, the ground beneath having been swept free of snow.

Blazing sconces lit the way. "Father Prior ordered them lit when we heard the bell and realised you were heading our way. Brother Thomas had been returning from visiting the sick when he spotted the coach stopped on the Peebles road." Mitchell felt he had to explain

"As Joe has probably already told you, we were stopped by a large bank of snow and ice and were waiting for the hearse to catch up." Brother Walter's voice held genuine grief as he replied to Mitchell.

"The arrival of Sir Ian's earthly remains. A sad sight indeed." Mitchell nodded in agreement and despite now being sheltered somewhat from the biting wind, he could feel the painful chill almost invading his very bones. He longed to be out of it.

"The ladies will have the guest-house to themselves. I'm afraid you and the other men will be in rather more austere quarters." Mitchell smiled slightly into the shadows. He knew the living quarters of the Priory very well indeed. The monk's idea of austerity and Mitchell's did not match. He once more thought of the back-breaking task of digging ground frozen solid in order to bury the dead in the Crimea, ground which one minute was your bed, the next your grave. The two Irishmen had already vanished by the time Mitchell had alighted from the coach. He would seek them out after dinner.

"Warm and water-tight, Brother Walter, that's all I ask."

"Then you will be more than satisfied. Dinner won't be for an hour or so for Lady Grant has expressed a wish for her husband's coffin to be placed in the Lady Chapel and that will take a little while to organise."

"A vigil is to be kept at all times then?" asked Mitchell surprised.

"Of course, as is our custom here at Collinge Woods Priory. Two brothers at all times. That way nobody falls asleep on the job," he added wryly. And theoretically, the body should be quite safe from harm in the Lady Chapel, more so than in the charnel house for it was little more than a storeroom with a simple padlock virtually anyone could break. Lady Grant was no more religious than her husband but she was definitely more wily. "No prayers, though, by request." Disapproval was rife in Brother Walter's voice. "Hungry?" he asked smiling once more.

"Brother, I could eat a horse." Mitchell said that with feeling.

"What happened to your head and face?"

"A snowball with a stone in it. The force threw me forward onto the iron rungs of the stagecoach. Street urchins apparently." Mitchell said that without feeling or, at least, conviction.

"I'll have Brother Max, our infirmarian, take a look at it. Splitting headache?" Brother Walter was used to Duncan Mitchell visiting the Priory as part of that extremely jolly outing of Lord Askaig's and Mitchell's lack of bonhomie right then was very evident.

"Headache to end all headaches. What I need is a good night's rest. Pain-free and full of sweet dreams, but right now, just a short nap in front of your kitchen fire?" Mitchell suggested hopefully.

"Be my guest, Mr Mitchell." And Lord Askaig's butler took full advantage of the invitation.

Mitchell stepped out into the moonlight once more, snow dancing and flurrying in the light breeze. But it seemed to be easing off yet again and a hard frost was inevitable. He stopped at the door of the guest-house and pulled on the rope attached to a small bell housed higher up in the two-storey building. The women had been housed there with the men settled between the two dormitories. The door was quickly opened and Maddy stood by at attention as Mitchell once more felt the enervating effects of sudden temperature change. It was a small parlour, log fire burning, apple-scented and easing its warmth throughout the room. He sat down by it and motioned to Maddy to sit opposite him. Maddy spoke first.

"If the ladies need anything, I'm to speak to the brother just inside the opposite door there, the refectory, says Brother Walter. I think that's his name. But we're not to use that door to go there. We're to use the one off the cloisters." Maddy knew Mitchell was familiar with the layout for she'd seen His Lordship and his entourage escape to the Priory often enough with Mitchell organising it all down to the last detail. She waited quietly for him to speak, the firelight flickering gently in the softly lit room. There was no sign of Lady Grant or the Cowans. They were evidently not expected for Maddy's feet were encased in hand-knitted boots. She followed his gaze and tucked her feet under the hem of her skirt. "My boots are drying next to the fire in my room - well, near it anyway. I won't need them till perhaps after dinner for I'm to eat in here said Lady Grant. Lady Grant said she would arrange for a monk to bring me some supper. I'm to make sure their luggage isn't tampered with." Mitchell nodded slowly. Maddy sniffed quietly. They both knew she was disappointed for she saw this trip as a great opportunity to show Mr Mitchell how good a detective she could be. She had to remember that she was still on trial with The Mitchell Detective Agency. Mitchell sensed her disappointment.

"I expect a key will perform that task just as well," Mitchell said. He needed Maddy free to roam, not imprisoned in the guest-house. Mitchell knew that both he and Maddy were servants but certainly not employed by Lady Grant. "I'll see one is delivered to her ladyship and also one to you," he added. "After dinner, perhaps, you might be willing to make some Lamb's Wool. Brother Conraitus is a lover of that ancient drink and Mrs Brady's version in particular." Maddy took the warning and grinned. She was nobody's fool. There was no way the monk would wheedle the full and secret recipe out of her but it would give her a chance to find out as much as possible about the Irishmen.

"Your boots, Maddy, didn't you bring another pair?"

"I left them in Crosteegan. I didn't think I'd be walking much. Mother knitted me these for the hospital."

"How's the ankle?" Mitchell was genuinely concerned.

"It's fine, thank you sir." Yes, he thought cynically, about as fine as my head. "And your head, sir?"

"Fine, thank you, Maddy." He sat back, closed his eyes and only wanted to rest. But there were arrangements to be made. The Mitchell Detective Agency was now on red alert. "Maddy, I need to know if there is any further attempt at communication between these two parties, that is the Irishmen who were on top of the coach and Lady Grant's party. Communication of any kind, Maddy, between any of them, for example meetings, notes, words, especially guarded words. Anything," he repeated, "I want to know who these men really are and why they are here. Do you understand?" Maddy nodded slowly and seriously as she had seen the butler himself do a hundred times in the course of his duties at Crosteegan Castle. He rose. "I'll have one of the brothers bring that key for you and one for the ladies. They can share. You keep yours at all times. If they quibble, tell them Lord Askaig's butler has given you orders you are expected to obey to the letter. Remember, Maddy, you answer to me, not to Lady Grant. I'll see you at dinner in the refectory."

Mitchell heard the door of the guest-house being closed firmly behind him and he did as promised and had keys delivered - one for Lady Grant and one for Miss Pearson. He decided to shortcut through the refectory as the door at the far end of the long, trestle-filled room led directly to the cloisters at the south end of which was situated the staircase access to the monks' main dormitory. A few slept in the smaller dormitory attached to the infirmary but Mitchell had been put in the large one that evening along with Joe Petherbridge and Captain Brogan.

"Mr Mitchell!" Mitchell stopped and looked back along the north side of the cloisters where some blue-white snow still lingered.

"Captain Brogan, sir, how may I help you?" The officer emerged from the shadows and approached Mitchell with a vigour Mitchell envied right then.

"I'm afraid that in the absence of Roderick Grant, I shall have to ask you if you would be kind enough to continue looking after the ladies' welfare on the next stage of our journey." Mitchell's heart sank but it was no more than he had expected. He had been hoping Roderick Grant would have fetched up at the Priory ahead of them, another victim of the weather. No such bloody luck, he thought savagely. His voice, now firm and respectful, belied his disappointment when he spoke.

"Of course, Captain Brogan, you have my help as long as you require it, sir. I expect though, Captain, that they are quite safe here."

"Do you?" asked the officer anxiously.

"Don't you?" asked Mitchell in alarm. Did Danny Brogan have more information than he had? Those alarm bells were doing Mitchell's headache no good at all. Brogan's face was unreadable in the shadows thrown by the flaming torches jammed into the sconces lining the ancient covered archway. Suddenly Brogan's fine features paled dramatically.

"This is a nightmare," he whispered and suddenly staggered slightly. But Mitchell's deft hand beneath his elbow steadied him almost immediately. Years of practice guiding inebriated guests, both male and female, down the sweeping marble staircase leading from Crosteegan's ballroom to one of its numerous lavatories came in handy occasionally.

"Captain Brogan, you talked of desecration. Can you describe to me exactly what damage had been done to the coffin?"

"The lid was partly smashed but not opened when we went to see to his removal from hospital this morning. But the coffin is solid oak - difficult to damage - and the person must have been scared off before he completed whatever it was he had decided to do." Brogan's face had taken on an even deeper pallor in the moonlight. The snow had ceased

"Captain Brogan, do you recognise the name Killelea? Or Fegarty? I think that they are in the coach-party. Could there be any serious connection to all of this with the Battle of Inkerman?" asked Mitchell. Suddenly Brogan slumped against a frost-coated pillar.

"The wall." Those two tortured words seemed to have been wrenched out of him. Brogan gave Mitchell a look of incredulity that turned inexorably to one of panic and terror. "Alan!" he suddenly cried out.

"Captain Brogan," Mitchell began but Danny Brogan had slipped silently into the folds of the soft snow still holding the half-swept passageway in its grip. Mitchell bent down to help then looked up at the infirmarian who had emerged silently from the church and now knelt by his side. He watched as the Priory's medical expert tended to the stricken officer.

"Dead?" Brother Max, the infirmarian, nodded as Mitchell spoke in shock. Mitchell walked slowly out into the searing chill of the snow-covered cloister garden.

Chapter 6

Mitchell's hunger had vanished and he merely toyed with the food on the plate before him at the long refectory table. He felt that Brogan had labelled the situation accurately for it was, indeed, a nightmare situation. He had already scanned that room in vain for Fegarty and Killelea. He turned to Brother Max sitting beside him.

"Are the other two men of our party not lodging with you here in the Priory?" Mitchell knew there was nowhere else but they seemed to have vanished. "The ones who came off the coach? I was told that they had already made arrangements to be dropped off here." Brother Max had a healthy appetite and it was some moments before he answered.

"Oh them. They fancied doing a bit of retreating before the excesses of Christmas, it seems. Got themselves robes. They're here in the refectory somewhere, I dare say." Brother Max's fork was waved vaguely over the brown-clad, cowled monks who filled the refectory along with the occupants of the stagecoach. Mitchell's headache increased but there was no point in pursuing the matter right then for Brother Max obviously knew nothing. "Have you formed an opinion, Brother Max, as to what actually carried the captain off? I take it the plague, foreign or home-bred, is a non-starter?" The monk had now by-passed the jelly in preference for a beaker of rough ale. He spoke after taking a deep gulp of it.

"Heart trouble." Mitchell nodded in agreement. A simple diagnosis was music to his ears. "That fool of an undertaker - coachman as he prefers to be called - says it was a broken heart because one of the ladies in Lady Grant's party had probably turned him down as a potential husband. He thinks."

"A broken heart," Mitchell repeated quietly, shaking his head and decided it was time for a breath of fresh air and a touch of sanity.

"Personally, Mr Mitchell, I'm a bit sceptical about the broken heart diagnosis as during the three times Captain Brogan has stayed here with his brother en route to the army camp at Dartmoor, he has suffered from rather alarming fainting spells. I expect it was his heart that finally failed without the aid of unrequited love. What's your interest in our retreat guests?" Brother Max was nobody's fool.

"I thought I recognised their voices. Old comrades. I passed out when the stone hit me and I faintly heard them asking if I was alright. I thought we'd met before but as I was persuaded to travel inside because of the head injury, I haven't had the chance to meet them."

"If you were old comrades, they'd surely have made a point of speaking to you when you'd regained consciousness."

Brother Max was invariably outspoken. Diplomacy was not in his make-up.

"I expect so," Mitchell agreed. "Think I'll give the mincemeat pies a miss."

"Me too. I'll make up a posset for the headache. Come over to the infirmary when you're ready. That concoction is guaranteed to make you sleep until just short of Judgement Day."

"I'll be over directly, Brother Max, and many thanks." They parted by the door at the far end of the west side of the cloisters and he smiled as he heard Brother Conraitus's voice behind the door leading to the kitchen.

Mitchell stood, deep in thought, in the silence of the night. Where did he himself fit into it all for he was certain coincidence played no part whatever in the day's events? He knew that he was still floundering around in a quagmire where danger was more sensed than tangible. He had been targeted with that stone and was well aware of it. Mitchell wondered if Maddy had winkled any information out of Lucy. He had hardly given her any guidance, poor girl. He hoped Maddy would have had the good sense to stay out of the freezing church as he silently made his way there and stood by Brother Walter's side. The monks were silently filing past. The procession about to begin. From his position by the western wall of the nave, Mitchell could look across and see the small party of ladies positioned before the biers now holding the coffins of Sir Ian and Captain Brogan. All was peaceful, all the ladies composed. No weeping, none expected. Where the hell was Roderick Grant? More to the point, where were Fegarty and Killelea? His eyes rested on the two monks kneeling by the coffin and sudden panic flooded through him.

"How were the monks for the Lady Chapel selected, Brother Walter?" His voice was strained but the monk put that down to fatigue and the effects of the head injury.

"Rotas. We have them for everything, for every possible occasion."

"No volunteering?" asked Mitchell. Brother Walter shook his head decisively and then smiled.

"No volunteers! The days of religious fervour in monasteries were well and truly over five hundred years ago. The monks all went on the Crusades and either didn't come back or the Black Death got them. Nothing disrupts the rota except a good excuse such as having dropped dead the day before."

"No last minute substitutes?"

"That vigil rota hasn't changed in over a year. Nobody has come and nobody has left. Only the brothers who have taken their final vows are allowed to participate. The grieving relatives don't want anybody just practising so to speak."

"So no last minute changes?"

"Duncan, this is a monastery not your Eddleston football team. By the way, our follower of your very own team, namely Brother Jude, has apparently discovered that his vocation has suffered a severe jolt. I wonder if he heard about Joe possibly bringing a party here three days ago and thought to take advantage of it. Instead of running away, perhaps he thought he'd try a less tiring method. But duty calls." Brother Walter left to resume his own duties as Father Prior's deputy as Margaret Campbell called to Mitchell.

"Mr Mitchell, may I have a word with you?" 'Duncan' had gone. For whose benefit had she used it in the coach?

"Mrs Campbell, I am at your service." He crossed to where Margaret Campbell now stood leaning slightly against one of the elaborately carved doors leading out into the snow-blanketed courtyard. He followed her out.

"There seems to have been an oversight regarding the small logs for the fire in our room - the one I share with Lucy. There are not enough of them to last the night and it would appear that we are to expect very low temperatures." Mitchell smiled.

"It would seem that the monk seeing to it must have been called away and has obviously simply forgotten to complete his task," he suggested.

"Quite so. Would you instruct Lord Askaig's servant to see to it?" Mitchell shook his head slowly.

"The girl is in no fit state to carry heavy loads, Mrs Campbell. She is recovering from an operation on her ankle and such a task would no doubt delay her recovery. I'll speak to Brother Walter. This has been a very distressing day for everyone. A warm room and a good night's rest will help all of us, Mrs Campbell." Margaret Campbell seemed in no hurry to move back into the warmth.

"We are all devastated by Captain Brogan's death." Margaret Campbell sighed as she spoke. But there was no-one more devastated right then than Mitchell and he felt truly ashamed when the 42nd football match jumped into his mind. "I believe his brother is staying at the Regent Moray in West Linton. He was intending going to Eddleston to pay his last respects to Sir Ian according to one of the monks who came from West Linton earlier this evening across the fields by sledge. Very dangerous but they made it. The roads in the area are extremely icy and it seems he's decided to remain there until there is a greater improvement in the roads. Looks like he was unaware that the general's body was still in Edinburgh. He left Edinburgh for Eddleston a few hours before us and managed to make it to West Linton. The Prior has made arrangements for him to be informed of his brother's death. That'll be another hazardous trip there and back for some unfortunate monks." Then again, thought Mitchell, that bit of self-sacrifice would probably earn them some kudos with the Prior. Margaret Campbell moved a little closer to him.

"You will remember to speak to whoever is in charge regarding wood for the fire, won't you please, Mr Mitchell?"

"I'll see to it at once." She smiled her gratitude and turned slowly and thoughtfully away. She hesitated slightly and he could almost hear the hardening frost form on the blue-tinged snow clinging to the arched tracery of the columns. Whatever she had been about to say went unsaid as she now obviously thought better of it.

"Goodnight, Mr Mitchell." He was alone once more but not for long.

"A word, please, sir," said Maddy. Mitchell leaned back against the inner wall, folded his arms and waited. If Mitchell were honest, Maddy's quicksilver mind both appealed to him and amused him. "Mr Mitchell, we're really short-staffed here, The Mitchell Detective Agency, I mean. Jude Donaldson's here," she added after a meaningful pause. Mitchell deliberately assumed a look of complete bafflement.

"And that's significant, is it?" Maddy's eyes dropped and she stared at the ground but not for long.

"That is my judgment, sir, yes. He's a monk here and now he wants to escape. I've had a preliminary word with him and he'll settle for a job at Crosteegan as an under-gardener in return for helping our - your - Agency in our - your - present case. He's also a first-rate footballer and Joe Petherbridge has offered him a job as an ostler in his stables if he'll play for his team. I thought maybe you'd want him for yours." As Mitchell remained silent, Maddy pressed on. "He says he hasn't actually signed up as a monk. He's here on a sort of look and see basis."

"And he's looked and doesn't like what he sees, is that it, Maddy?" Maddy nodded.

"That's about it. I'm sure that he would be an asset in our primary aim, Mr Mitchell.

"Which is? Remind me, Miss Pearson," said her boss.

"Keeping you alive, sir. I've got a brain, Mr Mitchell. I don't know the ins and outs of what's going on but I feel you're in deep trouble. You know we could do with another pair of male eyes and ears here in the Priory for I'm unable to use mine, as a female, at all times with the monks. I'm sure you'll have realised that it's a very delicate situation and if Mrs Brady." Maddy's voice tailed off for all of five seconds. "We're a gardener short anyway at Crosteegan and he's often helped on the estate in all departments including the stables from time to time."

"Bring him out, Maddy," said Mitchell for he knew she was right. He, too, had realised the advantages to be had from having an insider on the team. Mitchell heard Maddy laugh softly as she opened the kitchen door. A silent, cowled figure stole past her and sat beside Mitchell on the freezing ledge.

"Hello, Mr Mitchell."

"Jude Donaldson! Brother Jude!" said Mitchell shaking hands with the would-be errant monk.

"It should actually be Brother Rudolphus. Refuse to answer to that so they've all given up on it."

"Quite," said Mitchell who understood the Prior's dilemma. "Now Jude, I hear that you're about to climb over the wall." Mitchell knew Jude of old and tried hard not to laugh at the very idea he'd even walked through a monastery door.

"Climbing isn't for me, Mr Mitchell, no head for heights. Straight out through the door. All above board. Goodbye and all the very best." There were no dishonourable bones in Jude's body.

"Good riddance says Father Prior?" Mitchell suggested.

"Something like that," Jude admitted wryly.

"Been fighting again, have you?"

"Just a minor disagreement. Nobody's got a sense of humour in here."

"So why did you join up? The last I heard you were doing a bit of navvying on the railways."

"Got religion." This time Mitchell really did laugh.

"Still got it?"

"No. There's a lot I miss beyond the walls and that's putting it mildly, sir," said Jude

"And they miss you too, Jude." Mitchell bestowed a knowing smile on the young man.

"I'm descended from a long line of free spirits, Mr Mitchell. Some lucky girl will appear by the time I'm thirty-five and just ready to settle down." Brother Jude was all of nineteen.

"Lucky girl, eh, Mr Mitchell?" Maddy's scepticism was showing. Mitchell smiled in a pragmatic sort of way.

"Right Jude, a gardening job is yours plus an occasional one with The Mitchell Detective Agency if we're really desperate and right now that's exactly what we are."

"Done, Mr Mitchell, and no offence taken at that slight lack of faith in me. Maddy here's a witness to it all." Hands were shaken and Jude Donaldson rose to go in search of Father Prior and a one-way ticket to Eddleston.

"Jude, Maddy will keep you posted on our present case," said Mitchell. "Now the two men who joined the brothers today supposedly on retreat as lay persons. Keep an eye on them, will you?"

"Certainly, sir. Anything in particular that they might do that would be of interest?"

"Nothing. Just thought I might know them," said Mitchell.

"Well, I think I can set your mind at ease, Mr Mitchell. They definitely know you. Got a likeness of an army photograph propped up on a locker by one of their beds in the small dormitory. The three of you are in it. Six or seven soldiers in all standing in front of a tent. At Inkerman. It's written on it." Jude left unaware of the consternation he had caused. Time had never meant anything to him which was a bit of a drawback in a life strictly dominated by bells for worship and life in general. Mitchell tried hard to disguise his fear that this was indeed an Inkerman revenge reunion as he spoke to Maddy.

"Now, Maddy, your report please and come to the point fast. I'm beginning to feel rather cold." In fact, Mitchell's feet felt frozen solid and he wondered how long Lady Grant could stay on her knees in the insidious chill of the Lady Chapel.

"I've written it all down in my notebook, Mr Mitchell. I've got it here in my pocket." Mitchell held out his hand, took the little book and placed it in his travelling coat pocket.

"An oral report will do fine right now. I'll study the written one later. Now you sat between Miss Lucy Cowan and Mr Joe Petherbridge at dinner, I noticed. Take it from there, please. I'll interrupt when something needs either to be clarified or to be elaborated upon." He settled back against the wall, his eyes closed, his head throbbing dully.

"As you rightly said, sir, I sat between Lucy and Joe Petherbridge. Mrs Campbell sat on Lucy's right and she carried on a whispered conversation with her throughout the meal which was very well cooked if I might stray from the point a bit." Mitchell's stony look dared her to continue along that path and he waited for her to continue. Maddy took the hint. "I tried several times to talk to Lucy but she wasn't interested in talking to anyone but relatives. She smiled faintly a lot but ate little and said even less. In fact, she said nothing to me at all. She scratched a lot at the bandages on her wrists - you noticed them I take it, Mr Mitchell?" Mitchell had and was convinced that Lucy had tried to harm herself. No wonder, he thought, Margaret Campbell stuck to her like a leech.

"I noticed, Maddy. Lucy said nothing at all to you?"

"Nothing. Joe tried with his usual fund of silly stories."

"Stories that have you all giggling in the kitchen at Crosteegan?" he asked coldly. Maddy smiled broadly.

"Yes. You don't make us laugh, Mr Mitchell," she added and could have bitten her tongue at that hasty remark. Butler, skivvy, think before you speak, butler, skivvy, think before you speak. A mantra she should have remembered. It was some time before the silence between them was broken.

"Entertaining women in Lord and Lady Askaig's kitchen," said Mitchell thoughtfully. "Am I paid to do that, miss? Is that my primary reason for being at Crosteegan Castle?" The tone was mild but Maddy knew the truth of it all.

"No, sir." The strained silence told Maddy she had a lot to learn and that one occupation should never impinge on the other - ever!

"Go on with the report, please." Maddy seized the chance to be the ultimate detective

" I put one or two possibilities to Jude when I met him in the kitchen. He'd heard I was with you and figured I would gravitate towards the spuds and parsnips. Old habits die hard, he guessed. Jude just wanders about, Mr Mitchell. Between you and me and the grumblings I've heard fro some of the monks, I think the Prior will be glad to see the back of him. You know how to handle him so he'll be alright at Crosteegan. He was always around the estate anyway before his family moved to Wales. I reckon Jude was homesick for Eddleston. Needed a more permanent job and this was as good as anything else until he found one. Board and lodgings. Anyway, to get back to my report, once Joe had left, it was just Lucy Cowan and me. Is she really Lucy Campbell, do you think?"

"I've no idea." Mitchell had several ideas, none of which he was prepared to share with Maddy Pearson.

"Anyway, Mrs Campbell had told Lucy to stay exactly where she was. She would only be gone for a few minutes. Something about logs for the fire in their room."

"I know about that. She mentioned it to me," said Mitchell.

"I just started talking about Christmas at Crosteegan. That girl is so -so very."

"Fragile?"

"Yes, fragile. Somehow it just didn't seem right to be quizzing her. It would be like taking advantage of her, sir."

"It could save her life, Maddy, for all we know." Mitchell heard Maddy's sharp intake of breath. "I was talking about all the things we have at Crosteegan, about mistletoe, the Yule log, snow, robins, and holly that are sometimes on the cards Mrs Brady receives."

"Did she look interested? Or even begin to take the slightest interest?" asked Mitchell.

"She suddenly said, 'Who killed Cock Robin?'. You know, the old verse we all learn when we're young?" Had Mr Mitchell ever been young, Maddy wondered briefly.

"Who killed Cock Robin?" Mitchell repeated slowly.

"She seemed a million miles away. I don't think she even knew she'd said it aloud."

"Did she finish the verse?"

"Sort of, Mr Mitchell, in her own odd way. All she said was, 'I did.' Then she looked straight into my eyes and said again, 'I killed Robin.' I asked her if she meant Cock Robin and she just repeated 'Robin'. Then she began to tear at the bandages and Mrs Campbell appeared and took her away." Mitchell nodded.

"So who is Robin?" mused Mitchell. "Definitely not Sir Ian nor Captain Brogan. Brogan's first name was Daniel. All the officers always called him Danny. Danny Brogan of the 88th before he was transferred to the 42nd. Well, Maddy, there's only one way to find out."

"Do you want me to ask her?" Mitchell looked sternly at his skivvy cum trialist detective.

"No, Maddy. The girl is under enormous strain and whatever death she was involved in has obviously been twisted so much in her mind, anything she says is completely unreliable. If you'd choked on a chestnut at the refectory table, she'd be blaming herself for that, too. She's seen or heard something, maybe been involved in some capacity but whether or not she was responsible, deliberately or otherwise, these women will make certain nobody ever knows about it. Those bandages on her wrists peak of the terrible strain that young girl's under."

"So how will you find out?" asked Maddy.

"My only interest is in making sure she's not likely to repeat the act if she really did kill Robin. I'm to get you back to Crosteegan in one piece, still breathing, limping perhaps but still able to prepare vegetables. That is still my primary duty." Mitchell sighed. There were no Robins connected with Inkerman that he could recollect so any homicide extraneous to that could be dealt with by somebody else. Mitchell already had his hands full with what looked like somebody's weird fixation with some imaginary wrong in the Crimea.

"So we let a possible murderer escape." Mitchell had never liked drama. Maddy remembered that too late. He handed her back her unopened notebook.

"Yes," he said decisively, " unless we're being paid to do otherwise. So, as we are at the moment engaged in keeping my good self alive, whoever killed Cock Robin can feel free to eat as many crystallised chestnuts as he or she can stuff into his or her mouth by way of self-murder. We are not interested." For the first time Maddy really understood that it was a definite possibility that Duncan Mitchell might not survive it all.

"So it's a very real possibility - your dying, Mr Mitchell?"

"Yes, Maddy, and I've no doubt you will now pursue any would-be assassin assiduously because if there's no Mitchell, there's no detective job. The Mitchell Detective Agency will fold the minute I breathe my last." It was about to fold anyway for Duncan Mitchell was almost totally broke. His football club was soaking up all his savings, the match against the 42nd had been a kind of salvation waved tantalisingly before him only to be snatched away at the last minute.

"But why would someone want to kill you, sir?" It seemed to Mitchell that Maddy sounded more curious than distressed. Staff relations took a tumble.

"At the moment, I'm more interested in the 'how', but you do have a point." Mitchell lapsed into silence.

"Those two strangers." Maddy was convinced. "I'll bet it's them."

"Possibly - no, probably - yes. It has something to do with the Crimea but I have no idea what. There is nothing in my mind that could explain it. Maddy, go to bed. I'll talk to you in the morning," he ordered.

"You could be dead." Maddy always came straight to the point.

"And you out of a second job. There has to be a bright side in all of this." He'd looked in vain for that too. Maddy smiled with renewed confidence.

"There is," she said, "Brother Walkabout."

"Jude?" Maddy nodded.

"He'll be watching those two like a hawk. Maybe you could put him on the payroll, too, Mr Mitchell." He nodded thoughtfully at this suggestion before speaking.

"And I have another great idea, Miss Pearson. Maybe we could occasionally take some paying clients. Now that would be a novelty! Use their money to pay my staff of thousands instead of my own." Sarcasm was heavy as Mitchell spoke. He was always on the brink of financial disaster owing to his commitment to his football club. He still hoped it would make him a millionaire some day, preferably soon.

"We haven't discussed rates of pay yet, Mr Mitchell."

"Oh, neither we have. I wonder why? Could it be because as you seem bent on running things, I'm beginning to think you own the MDA and therefore you are the one responsible for paying lowly employees such as myself? Miss Pearson, do I so admire strong-minded women that I let them do my thinking for me?" Maddy shook her head.

"No, Mr Mitchell." In spite of it all, she did not doubt for a moment that Mitchell would survive this. In Maddy's eyes, Lord Askaig's butler was indestructible and breathtakingly resourceful. His only weakness - and Maddy had watched him very closely since he had started his detective agency - seemed to be Miss Eliza Cowan. Maddy had seen the way he had looked at her in Eddleston church. Well, Miss Cowan was too lacking in emotion to kill anybody, too wrapped up in being the perfect lady's maid. Hide-bound by duty, Mrs Brady had once said of her and she was right. Now that Mrs Campbell, she was more the type for Mr Mitchell, in Maddy's opinion. Much more - well, earthy, more appreciative of the man and less of the butler. A bit sharp-tongued on occasion but Mr Mitchell might find that a challenge. Maddy suddenly realised he was waiting for her to move. "Bed it is, Mr Mitchell. Goodnight, sir."

"Say nothing to Donaldson, Maddy."

"No need, sir, for his natural curiosity - being nosey is a family trait - will have already been on full alert."

"Unpaid alert."

"Quite so. Goodnight, sir." Mitchell stood in the freezing cold by the kitchen wall until she'd disappeared into the guest-house. The deep snow's surface now sparkled hard and blue in the flooding moonlight as a sharp frost began to bite. Mitchell felt deadly tired. The temptation to lie down and sleep the clock round was almost overwhelming but there was still one last thing he had to do.

He slowly opened the heavy door into the now-dimly lit church. The braziers at regular intervals along the walls had been allowed to die and the cold inside the building was, if anything, more severe than outside. He walked quietly but not silently along until he reached the Lady Chapel. His soft but deliberately audible footfalls were meant to warn Lady Grant and Eliza Cowan of his presence. He had no intention of frightening them. Two monks still kept vigil on their knees at the foot of the bier with Lady Grant, Eliza Cowan remaining seated a few yards behind them. Mitchell sat beside her and bent his head in solemn respect for a few minutes. Their meetings had been infrequent and very brief over the last ten years as Sir Ian and his family had spent most of each year in Florence. He glanced at Eliza Cowan and quashed all thoughts of personal longings, convinced himself they were all in the past. She had shown no interest in Lucy Cowan's distress or even common courtesy to Maddy inside the stagecoach. He now merely wanted her recollections of certain events. Nothing more. Not any longer. His voice when he spoke was pitched so that only she could hear.

"This is not helping, Miss Cowan." If she heard him, she ignored him. But Mitchell was not used to being treated thus by ladies' maids. He outranked them. He waited. Eliza Cowan was too well trained and they both knew it.

"It isn't within my power to stop it, Mr Mitchell." Her velvet voice was low, her head now turned slightly towards him.

"Have you tried?" He could have been speaking to Maddy and he knew he had overstepped the mark. Duty and pride, the Cowans double-edged sword, and he had questioned the value of both. The ice-blue eyes met his full on and her contempt for him was wordlessly conveyed. She slowly turned back to watching Lady Grant. "You have a duty to your niece, Miss Cowan," he continued.

"I shall bear that in mind, Mr Mitchell. Thank you for reminding me." He looked at the little purple bonnet with its lace and frivolous lavender ribbons and wondered if someone had chosen it for her.

"I know she slit her wrists." He waited but detected no reaction whatsoever to his words. "Do you not consider that a cry for help? Don't you consider it more important than sitting here watching a woman who has decided to deal with her husband's death, her own private grief, in her own private way? A woman who no longer needs your services tonight?"

"No I do not, Mr Mitchell." If she was shocked or surprised that Mitchell knew about Lucy, Eliza Cowan did not show it. Her self-righteousness was sickening and Mitchell wanted out of it. Even Margaret Campbell was more anxious to stop the girl talking than in comforting her. The Cowans were emotionally stunted, was that it?

"What do you remember of the Battle of Inkerman." he asked switching the topic suddenly. She responded after a few seconds.

"Inkerman? I expect there is some purpose in asking me that question but I not only fail to see what it could be, I also don't care to know." Mitchell ignored that statement.

"I'll repeat the question, Miss Cowan, and I expect an honest answer from someone who purports to be an honest woman.

What do you." But Eliza Cowan was quick to interrupt him this time.

"I did hear you, Mr Mitchell." Mitchell waited for her answer but when it came it was not the prevarication he had expected. "I remember nothing, nothing at all."

"But you were there with Lady Grant, watching from a short distance away. Sir Ian's proud boast was that the two of you ladies, his wife and her maid, were present together during the entire campaign and endured all its hardships."

"Then Sir Ian was mistaken for I was not with Lady Grant at Inkerman during the battle. Mr Mitchell, I was with you."

Chapter 7

Mitchell shivered so violently it woke him up. He was aware of movement about him, quick, purposeful, of men hurrying.

"A nightmare brought on by not sleeping in a bed. Move over, Mr Mitchell, you're in the way." Brother Conraitus's voice held a note of disapproval as he fired off instructions to the other monks helping prepare breakfast. Mitchell sat up, his mouth dry as a bone but his head perfectly clear and free of pain at last. Why had he slept here in the Priory kitchen instead of in the main dormitory? Laziness, probably, but that was not like him. He had been completely exhausted. What had he been doing? He had been talking to Maddy and Jude and. He stood up quickly as the memory returned.

"Thank you for your hospitality, Brother Conraitus. Must wash and see to my charges." He exited fast and took the steps to the dormitory two at a time. He had gone into the empty kitchen parlour the previous evening to think. The heat from the fire had given him what he'd badly needed - rest. Eliza Cowan's thunderbolt had shaken him to the core. Part of him had refused to believe a word of the references to Inkerman. Nothing of note bar the usual battlefield chaos and misery had occurred. But now he acknowledged that there was a massive blank about that in his memory, a blank that was liable to get him killed if he did not fill it in fast. But what had he really learned from her? Precisely nothing, well, not quite. They had both been there but not the way she had put it. With you, was what she had said. They had been together. Why? He had no recollection of ever meeting her before he had gone to work at Crosteegan Castle ten years previously and she was a neighbour's lady's maid. That had been years after Inkerman. His own regiment had not even taken part in the battle. Some of them had been seconded on a very temporary basis from The Black Watch, the 42nd, to the 88th. Days it should have been if he had not been wounded. As soon as he was better, it was back to the 42nd. At Inkerman, he had been caught up in an explosion and Margaret Cowan had nursed him back to health in the hospital at Scutari. But he had just been one of hundreds, perhaps thousands, she had helped. Yet, she remembered tending him. Duncan. Probably knew his name from village gossip for she now lived only a short distance from Eddleston and Lord Askaig's Crosteegan Castle. He plunged his hands and arms into the basin of ice-cold water supplied for ablutions. The pain shot through his entire body and he swore softly under his breath. Obviously, thought Mitchell sourly, when Lord Askaig visited the Priory, the austere rules went by the board and hot water was available to all at all times. He hoped the ladies were faring better. Fortunately, he had evidently been too fatigued to thrash about much and there was barely a crease in his clothes. A clean shirt did the trick and Mitchell was soon back in the refectory after a short, brisk walk through the crackling snow. The frost had set hard but a weakly sun had tentatively shed its rays about and Mitchell hoped for the beginnings of a thaw.

He looked about for Lady Grant. Where she was, so would be Eliza Cowan and this time his stunned silence would not allow her the opportunity to escape. Surely to god these women must have slept? They were nowhere to be seen and he knew that they would probably be in the Lady Chapel yet again and keeping their silent watch, stone cold along with Sir Ian, Danny Brogan and Mitchell's now-defunct insurance policy against bankruptcy. No football match, no money and Mitchell's savings were plummeting with all the teams debts assigned to him. Owning a football club was proving to be a very expensive hobby. He decided he would have a word with Brother Walter and see if, and perhaps when, the captain's brother might be expected and told diplomatically of the promised match. This was no time for diffidence, no time to defer to finer feelings. Mitchell quietly slipped into the refectory for breakfast.

Maddy was deep in conversation with one of the monks as Joe Petherbridge ate heartily on her other side. She smiled sweetly as she saw Mitchell enter and glanced at the empty space opposite her. Mitchell silently accepted the invitation from Madeleine Pearson to her employer, Duncan Mitchell of The Mitchell Detective Agency, and mentally noted that Madeleine, her preferred Agency name, and Jude had the makings of a good team. He filed that thought away for later consideration as Jude Donaldson ate his porridge with thick cream beside Michael Fegarty, playing the innocent at large and making a very convincing job of it. Fegarty looked bored to death.

"Did you have a good night's rest, Duncan?" Fegarty asked smiling as Mitchell sat down.

"That I did, Michael. And you?" The jousting had begun.

"The same. Pity about the cold water but us old soldiers think nothing of that, am I right?"

"Absolutely. And Dominick?"

"Haven't seen him as yet this morning but I expect he did," said Fegarty. Joe Petherbridge swallowed his mouthful of scrambled eggs before explaining to Mitchell.

"Seems there was a mix-up with the surnames on my list, Duncan," he said as Maddy passed him the salt. "Should have read Mr M Fegarty and Mr D Killelea."

"No harm done I expect," said Mitchell taking some crusty bread from the large basket before him as he spoke and buttering it thoughtfully. Petherbridge had decided he was still hungry and he helped himself to some porridge. He devoured it after liberally dousing it with salt and milk The chill had sharpened all appetites, it seemed. "Now when did we last meet, Michael?" Mitchell asked.

"Well, now, Duncan, there you have it for it's all a bit hazy. I expect it is to you, too." Mitchell nodded.

"Just a gap in my memory that I didn't know I had," he agreed.

"Beginning to come back, is it? They say a sudden shock can take the memory away but that it can also work both ways. Takes it away and brings it back. Or maybe there are some things best forgotten and the brain just opts out. No fuss, no bother, no nightmares."

"I've heard that," said Mitchell, nodding thoughtfully. "That's the trouble with being quickly switched from one regiment to another at the beginning of a battle. No time to get to know people, no reality except what's happening right by your side. At least I knew you and Dominick reasonably well from previous engagements."

"Still, you came out of that particular one with our regiment pretty well, though, didn't you? Got back to the 42nd and all your mates eventually."

"I suppose you could say that. No memory of it, only the hospital afterwards." Mitchell glanced at Maddy. "Yesterday's news now to these young people," he said and shrugged. "Are you on your way to the Lady Chapel? Paying your last respects to Sir Ian, Michael?" Fegarty nodded.

"And to Captain Brogan, too, now, Duncan. I'm told his brother was a regimental hero at Inkerman. One of your lot. Quick transfer - like yours. Fought the battle, transferred back." Mitchell shook his head.

"I don't remember any Brogan in the 42nd," said Mitchell thoughtfully.

"Well, you wouldn't for he's his half-brother. Same mother, different surname." Mitchell waited for the name but Fegarty suddenly rose. "Now, I must have a word of condolence with Lady Grant." Mitchell watched him stroll slowly out of the refectory. So whose mangled remains had they buried on the morning before the actual battle? The old story of switching identities then deserting, thought Mitchell sourly.

"Joe, you ferry people back and forth all the time, Peebles, Eddleston, Edinburgh. Any army officers related to Captain Brogan ever visit while Captain Brogan was staying at the Manor in Eddleston?"

"Now Duncan, that's a hard one. Related to Captain Brogan? I'm not at all sure there was one. Not another Brogan as I recollect." Mitchell quickly explained.

"He wasn't called Brogan. Mr Fegarty said he was his half-brother, different fathers. Two husbands," Mitchell added and coloured slightly, hoping Maddy had not been listening. He was making a right hash of it and put it down to the head injury.

"Let me think," said Joe.

"The only other thing Fegarty said about it was that he was in my old regiment," Mitchell said. That did the trick.

"I remember now there was one who was a regular visitor from The Black Watch. Was a great favourite of the general's. That would be Major Sinclair. So he's Captain Brogan's half-brother? Well, well, well. Different personalities by a mile," laughed Joe Petherbridge.

"Major Alan Sinclair?" Mitchell laughed too. "Well what do you know! Sod-them-all Sinclair! Craziest officer in the Black Watch."

"Good officer?" asked Petherbridge through another slice of bread and butter.

"Great! Very young then but fearless. Not reckless, though, just fearless. Very canny. Never took unnecessary risks with his men. Specialised in secret missions, those in the know hinted and I could well believe them. I thought he'd gone to run the family estates when his time was up." Petherbridge shook his head.

"Still on the strength. As a matter of fact, he's expected here anytime. Walking here through the snowdrifts from West Linton. By the way, Brother Walter says young Roderick Grant has fetched up there, too, from the opposite direction and seems he's decided that he'll just wait at the Regent Moray till we come. But the captain's brother will be here directly. He's planning to set out after breakfast. Another of the monks made it there and back on the sledge late last night. Seems the Prior's having fits about the reported behaviour of the stranded monks so he was determined to let the major

59

know and also to convey to his off-the-lead monks that retribution awaits them here."

"Joe, I was just wondering exactly who was at Inkerman. I mean of the people who are here at the Priory apart from the monks, of course. Seems like a reunion for some. I mean there was Miss Cowan, Lady Grant, Mrs Campbell, me, Fegarty and Killelea, Sir Ian and you, Joe." Mitchell knew in his heart of hearts that Fegarty and Killelea were obviously not really at Inkerman at all having taken their leave before it all began.

"I was certainly in the area with my ship as you know," said Petherbridge, "but before it all kicked off. The Naval Brigade and all our ships were standing off in the Sevastopol Roadstead but the fog was so dense, we couldn't sail to be with the rest of the transports off the Alma. Some of us managed to row ashore into Careenage Bay in the fog with some boxes of ammo and we hauled them up the Careenage Ravine. Thick fog and we just missed six thousand Russians we were told later. We ran into some of our soldiers, handed over the boxes and didn't wait around for them to sign delivery slips. Met a few more soldiers by the water's edge and some of them fancied a lift out of it. Deserters. But we were having none of it. We were all professionals, in it for better or for worse. When the crunch comes, you rely heavily on your mates. We headed back the way we had come, or as near as we could tell, and reached the safety of our ship after one hell of a struggle to find her in the suffocating fog. So, although I was there, I really wasn't in a manner of speaking. But right now, I must be going. One or two things to attend to plus the horses." Mitchell drank his coffee deep in thought and Maddy toyed with the remains of her toast.

"So much for Inkerman, Mr Mitchell. Seems like it was all a coincidence. Do we start all over again?" Suddenly Mitchell shook his head.

"I don't believe anything has really changed, Maddy."

"It still doesn't make any sense to me, though, sir." Maddy straightened up.

"You know what? It does now to me, Maddy, or at least it's beginning to. But I have to speak to Miss Cowan again and straight away at that. Wait in the cloisters and keep an eye out for Jude. I saw him leave the refectory before Fegarty. Maybe he has an idea where Killelea is."

"I had a word with him half an hour ago," said Maddy and Mitchell knew Jude was on the case.

"Reported to base, did he?" Mitchell tried hard to bury a smile in a studious look at the huge porridge bowl. He was rewarded with a bout of stony silence. He rose and left still hungry.

Mitchell stopped for a few moments in the cloisters, his breath crystallising in the raw, cold air about him. Although no great admirer of nature, he admitted to himself that the scene before his eyes was perfect for Christmas. Holly bushes, ivy, mistletoe and Robin Redbreast hopping through the greenery. Another enigma. Who killed Cock Robin? Who had Robin actually been? He decided to leave it there. It was not his problem. Eliza Cowan had dropped that bombshell about being with him then had moved off while he was still in shock. Short of following her into her bedroom, he had been able to do nothing until now. She and Lady Grant must have risen well before first light, eaten and then gone to the Lady Chapel. Probably all four of them would be there for Maddy had not said otherwise. He would speak to Eliza Cowan and then double back and learn what Maddy had got from Jude.

The church was now being cleaned, after the latest office of the day had ended for the monks of Collinge Woods Priory. The long nave was being swept and the advent candles trimmed, pewter cleaned and brass polished. The smell of beeswax filled the air. The braziers were once more lit all round at regular intervals along the walls and they had taken some of the chill from the air.

"Mr Mitchell! Duncan!" Mitchell waited for Brother Walter to reach his side. "Sleep well?" the Prior's deputy asked.

"Like a Yule log, Brother Walter." He hoped his sojourn in the kitchen was not common knowledge but he doubted it.

"So I heard."

"I expect it was the crack on the head. Those last few yards just seemed beyond me." Mitchell smiled wryly as he offered this feeble explanation. Brother Walter shook his head.

"I don't know what that girl of yours put in the spiced ale, Lamb's Wool she calls it, but the brothers who sampled it say they had the best night's sleep of their lives."

"She was probably a bit heavy-handed with some of the herbs. Nothing deliberate. She tends to be over-enthusiastic in whatever she decides to do. She's still learning."

"Then she has plenty of volunteers to sample her next batch of it. Brother Jude is leaving us - for ever and a day, we hope. He'll be going with your party in or on Joe Petherbridge's stagecoach."

"Do I hear sighs of relief all round?" Mitchell suggested. Brother Walter smiled broadly in agreement.

"More or less. Tells us he's settling down in Eddleston. Nice little cottage and an equally nice little wife seeing to his every need - eventually. I think the lad just misses his freedom. Got the wanderlust, not religion. He's a free spirit and god help any wife he does take."

"Brother Walter, Jude has no intention of subscribing to the 'wee humble cottage' life. He's young and a job on the estate and maybe a game of football is, I'm told, what he wants right now."

"He's a clever lad, Duncan. High-spirited but nobody's fool." Was Brother Walter warning him, wondered Mitchell. Don't underestimate your new employee? What on earth had Jude got up to in the Priory - or maybe outside it when he should have been inside it? Was that the problem? Containing him? Mitchell smiled for the monks did not have Madeleine Pearson on the team. Maddy's betrothed, Davie Elliott, was Mitchell's star player.

"I've seen him with our young skivvy," said Mitchell. "She's got him well under control. I think he was at school with one of her brothers. She's got six of them, I believe. Knows how to handle young men."

"And how is the Agency coming along?" The exaggerated innocent look told Mitchell all he needed to know. Brother Walter missed nothing.

"Expanding as far as personnel is concerned." Short and to the point.

"I thought so. Now, Duncan, try and get Lady Grant to ease up on the watch. She's making my monks look positively frivolous." Brother Walter shook his head in resignation and moved over to supervise the monk cleaning the rood screen. Mitchell stood for a moment watching the scene being played out in the Lady Chapel and wondered again what Sir Ian would have made of it all. A less religious man would have been hard to find. But the soldier doted on his wife and would have thought lying in state a small price to pay for her peace of mind. She was on her knees yet again, flanked by two monks, who were no doubt trying to look more devoted than the widow in front of Brother Walter, though how that could be achieved in somewhat threadbare robes on a freezing, flag-stoned floor defeated Mitchell. His look as always finally rested on the calm, composed figure of Eliza Cowan sitting completely still behind the widow and beside her sister and niece. Lucy looked completely exhausted although the hour was still early. She was probably a year or two younger than Maddy but their zest for life simply did not stand comparison. Mitchell felt his anger towards Eliza Cowan surge yet again. At that moment, she turned her head and looked directly at him. A whispered word to her sister and then she rose and exited the church. He knew he would find her waiting for him in the cloisters. More of the same? He hoped not and braced himself for the chilly air and even chillier attitude of the woman towards him.

The ice-blue eyes now lingered on him.

"If you have any questions, Mr Mitchell, I'll do my best to answer them." She did not add that she knew nothing but it was implied just the same.

"Thank you for your time, Miss Cowan." She shivered slightly but stood resolutely, now gazing out across the snow-blanketed quadrangle, silent monks gliding past occasionally on the far side of the cloisters in the framing fretwork of the ancient arches. He waited. She finally turned to him again.

"You want to know exactly what, Mr Mitchell?" She looked tired.

"Perhaps a seat on the wall bench," he suggested.

"Is your head still hurting?" she asked not moving.

"Yes." She would give in and sit for him but not for herself. He felt her need to be gone from there despite her apparent ease and control. Anxious to be back hovering solicitously about her employer. Duty! Was there anything else in her life? Mitchell felt shame flood through him. Who was he to try and order other people's lives? They sat down side by side and he was glad he did not have to look directly into those deadened eyes. But the softness of her voice as she spoke turned the screw in him yet again. Would he ever be free of her?

"There would appear to be a problem I'm not aware of." She stopped, removed her gloves and slowly rubbed her hands together, a peridot in a small gold ring sparkling in the pale sunshine seeping into the cloisters. She suddenly put the gloves back on. "Despite what you think, Mr Mitchell, Cowan women are neither stupid nor useless. My sister was nursing nearby and my brother had been an army surgeon in the Crimea. I knew the regiment well. I did not feel alone out there at any time that day."

"But you said you were not really there."

"I meant that I know nothing of what you were doing or of the battle itself. I didn't hear a single shot fired except from some way off, not in my immediate vicinity. I was removed from the scene almost as soon as it began, as were you."

"I remember absolutely nothing of it either," said Mitchell almost to himself.

"One thing you might possibly remember, Mr Mitchell, was that there was a dense fog at Inkerman that day. I was sent on an errand by Lady Grant and suddenly I found myself in the middle of the actual battlefield. My pony bolted as I tried to lead it through some bushes and I found that I was amongst men of the 88th who had been ordered to the Front and simply couldn't find it because of the fog. I decided I might as well stay with Sir Ian's men who knew me as perhaps wander in amongst the Russians who were close by."

"God Almighty," breathed a shocked Mitchell as Eliza Cowan spoke of her ordeal without any great feeling. She must have been terrified but she had kept her head just as her sister had done when seeing the gut-wrenching injuries before her. "When exactly did you and I meet up, Miss Cowan" he asked quietly.

"I crouched in the lea of a wall as the fog once more had left me alone. I then heard Major Sinclair shout, then you, I suppose. Suddenly you were all there, climbing the wall. The next thing I remember is waking-up in a mud-filled ditch with you beside me. It seems there had been an explosion as you reached the top of the wall. There was blood everywhere. I thought your head had been blown off. Obviously I was mistaken, Mr Mitchell," she added softly and suppressed a smile.

"And were you badly hurt?" he asked her.

"I was sent home but returned a year or so later. I must go now. My presence is required by Lady Grant's side." Mitchell, the butler, deftly opened the heavy oak door of the church for her and she silently resumed her place at her employer's side.

Mitchell's eyes caught sight of Brother Walter as he approached along the nave.

"Need a breath of fresh air, Duncan." His gaze followed Mitchell's. "I don't suppose that vigil will do them any harm, Duncan, if they don't actually catch pneumonia. Grief makes people do odd things. We're expecting Major Sinclair later this morning if he can battle his way through. A few mile-high snowdrifts are nothing in the way of obstacles to the major. He'll perhaps be able to assert a bit of influence and common sense into things." Brother Walter was obviously not used to someone else, especially a woman, dictating things in his all-male domain. The Grant party would be hustled out of the door post haste. Major Sinclair's presence would solve it all as far as Mitchell, too, was concerned. It was good to get that confirmation for that was the one important piece of information that Eliza Cowan had given him that the explosion had wiped from Mitchell's memory. Alan Sinclair had definitely been present that day when it had all happened at Inkerman and he was now coming to claim his half-brother's body. A sudden feeling of dread slithered like a snake over Mitchell's body.

"Brother Walter," he said quickly, " there's no need for Major Sinclair to make that trip. Travelling here in these conditions can be very dangerous. I'll see that both Sir Ian's and Captain Brogan's remains are safely conveyed to Eddleston until the weather clears enough for Captain Brogan's family's wishes to be known and carried out. The major could meet us there."

"A nice gesture, Duncan, but too late. The major is determined to set out on foot after a night's rest, or so he said to one of the brothers. Probably already has."

"Sounds like he hasn't changed." Mitchell's voice was steady and deliberate but his mind was in overdrive. What had he just realised? Major Sinclair had now been added to the Inkerman list. Was he another potential victim? Who had all been there? Sir Ian, Major Sinclair, Joe Petherbridge, Killelea and Fegarty and, of course, Mitchell himself. Of that group, Sir Ian had already died within the past few days plus the mysterious death of Captain Brogan which could potentially have been a way of luring Major Sinclair into the web. Had natural causes beaten them to it? Assuming

Killelea and Fegarty were the main suspects with Margaret Cowan Campbell somehow involved with them, that only left the major, Joe and himself. Eliza Cowan and Lady Grant were not involved in this revenge conspiracy, he decided and Margaret Campbell only because Maddy thought there was a deep meaning in a nod from Fegarty or Killelea. Even Petherbridge was only mildly so because he had never actually made it into the thick of things, only lugged some boxes of ammunition up a hill from the bay and then scampered back to his ship on the double.

"Brother Walter, if, when he arrives, Major Sinclair can persuade Joe Petherbridge and Spanswick's driver to leave straight away, you'll be able to rest easy. Father Prior will have all his side chapels just as he likes them, candle-lit and empty." Mitchell wanted all of them out of there. Killelea and Fegarty would be thwarted for Mitchell was now convinced that the Priory had been deliberately chosen as the place for revenge. Why, he did not know.

"It won't be that simple, I'm afraid, Duncan, for we are now waiting for another coachman. Joe Petherbridge got in the way of a falling hammer not twenty minutes ago. Mr Killelea was kindly helping mend the roof after some slates had become dislodged in the snowstorm. Frozen hands always lead to accidents themselves and unfortunately Joe passed under as the hammer slipped from Mr Killelea's hand." Mitchell forced himself to speak.

"How is he?" Mitchell's twisted stomach told him the answer even before the look on the monk's face did.

"That's what I was coming to tell you but you were with Miss Cowan."

"How is he?" Mitchell repeated starkly.

"Dead."

Chapter 8

Mitchell's sluggish brain could barely take this news in.

"Dead!" His voice was hardly above a whisper. Brother Walter shrugged.

"Well, near enough. His head's lucky it's still on his shoulders but his jaw's broken. I doubt if he'll ever talk sense again if he survives this. Seems he must have glanced up, saw the hammer fall and managed to move very slightly to his left. Unfortunately, he tripped and his face crashed off the flagstones round by the Prior's own lodgings. Brother Max has him in the infirmary and he'll stay there until we can move him in comfort to hospital in Peebles. Once the experts have given him their verdict, we'll have him back here." Fear chilled Mitchell's spine as Brother Walter spoke. What had Petherbridge actually done at Inkerman and to whom? Nothing, as far as either Joe or Mitchell himself knew. Mitchell's head was being shot through with pain yet again and he wanted very badly to lie down, stop thinking and go to sleep. But not forever and it was that thought that kept his brain turning over. Now only Major Sinclair would be able and willing to give him the answers he needed. It was time Maddy earned her money. Mitchell conveniently forgot he was not paying her anything. Jude, he decided, could use that quicksilver brain of his for once instead of his feet.

"Is Joe receiving visitors?" The monk shook his head.

"I'll let you know if and when Joe's out of danger, Duncan" The disapproving look was there. Something was going on but the monk could not figure it out.

Mitchell walked determinedly to the kitchen parlour. Maddy was seated before the roaring fire being waited on hand and foot, Brother Conraitus communicating with her through the open door into the kitchen itself. She quickly leapt to her feet when Mitchell appeared.

"Good morning, Mr Mitchell. Mr Mitchell is here, Brother Conraitus, and he's had virtually no breakfast I noticed." There was a small ash table where Conraitus obviously studied his accounts. Mitchell sat down on the cushioned seat and eyed Maddy solemnly. "There's nothing Mr Mitchell doesn't like or won't eat." Her veiled order was duly acknowledged by Brother Conraitus. Maddy had obviously been both an admirer of his cooking and a contributor to his ever-growing store of recipes.

"Now, Maddy," Mitchell began but was interrupted immediately.

"Sit down, please, Mr Mitchell. Five minutes and you'll be hungry no more. Brother Conraitus himself has offered to cook your breakfast and he is a wonderful cook as we all know. Mrs Brady says so too. Help yourself to bread and cheese. It's by the candle-store shelf." Maddy had obviously had a good look round and smiled as she waited for him to begin.

"Maddy, have you anything to report before I issue your orders for the day. I already know that Mr Petherbridge has met with an accident." He cut himself a small wedge of cheese as he spoke.

"I thought you might for Brother Conraitus said that Brother Walter was looking for you, you being one of Joe's passengers and sort of in charge of everything now that Captain Brogan has passed over."

"He hasn't passed over, Maddy, he's dead."

"But he has passed over the Great Divide, Mr Mitchell, the one between us and, well, them that's passed over it." It seemed that Maddy Pearson had very definite views on that subject.

"He's still dead, Maddy, whichever way you look at it and we're in a bit of a fix because of it."

"How so, Mr Mitchell?" she asked frowning.

"Because I cannot be in two different places at the same time."

"You mean the hearse and the coach?"

"Exactly."

"I see your point. But the coach will be going nowhere now that Mr Joe Petherbridge is no longer fit to drive it."

"His guard could and would take over as far as I know but that coach is going nowhere until the roads hereabouts have improved and that will not be before tomorrow at the earliest. So, in the meantime, we are stuck here with what could be a very tricky and ultimately for me, a fatal problem."

"I'm watching out for you, sir, and so is Jude Donaldson. He sees and hears everything."

"And knows nothing. How is that possible, Maddy?" The girl shook her head.

"I've told him to tell me what he hears and I'll decide what it means. He is really very clever, Mr Mitchell. It's just that it will take him some time to get used to acting on what his brain is screaming is important. It's attitude, Mr Mitchell. He's too lackadaisical but that'll change with a bit of instruction from me, sorry us, I mean you." Maddy's solemnity was acknowledge by Mitchell.

"Do you think it'll work - this business of he hears, he sees, but you decide?" Maddy had fooled nobody. "Will we get much-needed results while a complete fool is still evolving into a genius?" asked Mitchell sceptically. Maddy nodded vigorously.

"Yes, because you see, he's really as sharp as a tack but he plays the fool to his own advantage. He stops short of letting a girl do his thinking for him so we now have his pride as well as his brain fully engaged." Mitchell allowed himself a broad grin as he bent over the loaf of oatmeal bread before him. "Cut it as thick as you like, Mr Mitchell, because it's the best. Brother Conraitus makes a few specially for the monks who help in the kitchen." Mitchell did as Maddy had suggested and also helped himself to the Priory's own honey. He took a satisfying bite and immediately felt he could begin to cope. The bacon and eggs placed before him by Brother Conraitus sent his taste buds into overdrive before he had even picked up his cutlery.

"Report, please, Maddy." Sight and smell were almost as important as taste and he could listen just as well as he ate.

"It's all in the book." Maddy produced the notebook from her skirt pocket.

"Good." Mitchell took it and placed it in his travelling coat pocket yet again. This had all the makings of a future ritual. He wondered if, years down the line, he would eventually open it and find it blank.

"You prefer a spoken report, Mr Mitchell?" He nodded.

"Oral is the word, Maddy, not spoken. Same thing though," he muttered truthfully. The eggs were seriously good, yolks just set with just a touch of salt and pepper which he himself had added sparingly. He helped himself to another thick slice of the newly-baked bread. Maddy deftly slipped the Priory marmalade to within his reach as she began her oral report. Rough cut, he noted, just the way he liked it. He took the hint from Maddy's continued silence and halved the slice with her.

"Many thanks, Mr Mitchell."

"Please sit down." He waited for her to settle, accepted another two rashers of bacon from Brother Conraitus and listened carefully to his unpaid, not-as-yet-contracted employee's impeccable, oral report.

"As you know, sir, the two strangers, Fegarty and Killilea, are here on retreat as well as attending the funeral in Eddleston eventually although retreat is not actually allowed at the moment."

"And they have opted to wear the habit," said Mitchell. Maddy nodded.

"This is the first time they've opted to wear them. They usually wear their own clothes."

"So they've been here before?" asked Mitchell thoughtfully.

"They're stone-masons to trade. They do the rounds of abbeys and priories and private residences occasionally."

"A good, steady living. Go on, Maddy."

"I don't know anything about their lives away from here. Nobody does because nobody's been interested enough to ask," she said. Mitchell nodded slowly.

"Well that makes sense. As long as they do a good job and their prices are reasonable, I'm sure they just let the two of them get on with it." He drank his coffee absently, already deep in thought, trying to tie it all in, looking for some kind of connection, a thread that ran through it all. "Any more, Maddy?"

"Bits and pieces." She finished her bread and marmalade and watched Mitchell as he topped up his coffee.

"Would you like some?" Maddy shook her head.

"No thank you, sir."

"Then continue, please." Maddy did so.

"At the moment any work they do in the Priory is free as they are simply here on a sort of holiday. Retreating from the world for a few days while they are here to renew their spiritual energy, says Brother Conraitus."

"Some hope," said Mitchell flatly. He was now convinced that the pair of them had somehow helped Danny Brogan on his journey across the River Jordan in order to lure Major Sinclair to Collinge Woods Priory. "I think we know what their eventual goal is but not why they are trying to achieve it."

"True, Mr Mitchell, and that's what I told Jude. I told him your agency only employs folk who can get past the obvious."

"You did, did you?" Mitchell was impressed.

"Yes."

"He wants to be on the payroll now?" Mitchell asked in measured tones.

"Yes."

"Continue. I assume - I hope - there is more," said Mitchell.

"It's all in the notebook." He passed it back to her and she put it once more into her skirt pocket. "Jude sat beside Killelea in the refectory at breakfast before you and Mr Fegarty came in, sir. Likes to rise early. Jude does, I mean. Well, actually he made it look as though he was sitting beside one of the other brothers and was confiding in him his plan to leave the religious life. Said he fancied joining the army. Or the marines, even, the Naval Brigade. That way you get the best of both worlds, he said. Talked his usual load of nonsense. It lets the others feel superior and then they pile in with advice he says." Mitchell made a mental note to button his lip when Jude was about for pride made even the most cautious foolhardy. "The brother he was talking to, though, just said he'd be glad to see the back of him. Jude was a little hurt," said Maddy sympathising with her colleague. Monks should be more charitable, she thought.

"Some people always give frank opinions, Maddy, but it seldom wins them any friends. Frankness is not always the best route to travel in the detective business and in fact it is very often the worst, possible choice. Bear that in mind."

"I'll do that, sir." He smiled at her and polished off the last of his very good coffee. He thought she might have jotted down that little tip in her notebook. "I've made a mental note of it, Mr Mitchell." That brought him up with a jolt. He had always fancied he was an enigmatic type of man and the idea that even Lord Askaig's skivvy could read him like a book was rather unsettling to say the least. But he consoled himself with the belief that Maddy Pearson was a very exceptional and astute girl.

"Anything else?" This was getting them nowhere but he had enjoyed a wonderful breakfast. No kidneys, kippers or kedgeree on offer as they always had at Crosteegan but enough choice and of a quality to satisfy a hungry man used to superior cooking.

"Killelea said to Jude to avoid the marines. They were the scum of the earth."

"Did he now?" Mitchell was suddenly intrigued. "And?"

"Jude played the part of the not-so-bright and unworldly monk. Said he had an uncle who'd once seen a detachment of marines coming back from some war or other landing at Plymouth. Didn't look as smart as the Highlanders in their kilts but wearing good solid gear just the same." Mitchell was wearing his superior, swaggering smile as Maddy spoke. "And the stories they told in the public houses and inns you wouldn't believe, said Jude. They were amazing, he said, all wide-eyed. No, he insisted, it was still the Naval Brigade for him. But where to join up? That was the problem. Not easy to find out when he was virtually locked up here in the Priory, Jude moaned. Then Killelea said that if he fancied sending other men back to their deaths, then the Naval Brigade was definitely his best bet."

"Sending men to their deaths?" Bells were ringing in Mitchell's head.

"His exact words, Mr Mitchell, according to Jude. Jude pretended to be puzzled and asked Killelea where the recruiting sergeant might be found. Killelea said he was to ask Joe Petherbridge for he had been a first-rate member of that Brigade. Had even been at Inkerman. Killelea sounded very sour."

"And now Joe's dead or as good as," mused Mitchell.

"Has he crossed over yet?"

"That crossing's getting a bit clogged up right now, Maddy." Maddy did not laugh nor even smile slightly. "Maddy, in oral reports you may use the phrase 'crossed over' but in written ones, the word you will always employ will be 'dead'. Understood?"

"Yes, Mr Mitchell." Mitchell reckoned that the notebook could now be binned.

"So what we have is Killelea more or less saying that Joe Petherbridge had somehow sent someone back up a hill to his death."

"How could he have done that?" Mitchell now knew that there was a distinct possibility that the soldiers Joe had refused to let on his boat had in fact been Killelea and Fegarty for they had definitely deserted that day. They had obviously switched identities with two dead bodies hours before the battle had taken place, two men whom Mitchell had helped bury. Now who else could have been with them but had died there in that battle and was so important to them that fifteen years later they were still trying to avenge his death?

"But now Joe Petherbridge is out of it since Killelea's hammer fell on his head," said Maddy.

"Joe's not on the deceased list yet, Maddy, but I think he was meant to be. Of course, this is all just speculation."

"Until we find who's controlling it all," Maddy suggested.

"That would definitely change things. Joe will be quite safe, though, for Brother Max will be watching him like a hawk."

"No visitors allowed, Mr Mitchell, and that's a fact." Brother Conraitus joined them as he spoke and placed a plate of buttered cheese scones for them on the table. A silent brother appeared with a jug of ale then left as silently as he had appeared.

"Keep an eye on the custard, Thomas!" Brother Conraitus instructed the receding back. He turned his attention once more to Mitchell. "I tried taking Joe Petherbridge some thin but nourishing soup but I got short shrift from Brother Max." Maddy's diplomatic skills came to the fore and succeeded in smoothing the monk's ruffled feathers.

"Brother, he had just finished a huge breakfast in the refectory. A tribute to your cooking, of course. Joe won't need feeding for days, if he lasts that long," said Maddy. The monk waved away all concern.

"He'll last. He's only badly bruised his face or something like that. Practically got off scot-free when you think of what might have happened if that hammer had actually hit his head full on from that height. Granted I'm no medical man," Brother Conraitus added as an after-thought. "I'll fatten him up when we get him back from Peebles. Might not even need to go there, in my opinion. Rest and good food should be quite sufficient, I said to Brother Max, but he just threw me out of the room - physically threw me out." Mitchell and Maddy both made consoling noises to assuage the monk's pride. "Now tell me, Mr Mitchell, did I hear Dominick Killelea's name mentioned as I came in from the kitchen?" Mitchell nodded and dutifully drank his ale which was exceptionally good. "I knew his cousin, of course, we all did."

"His cousin?" asked Mitchell quietly and even Maddy refrained from her usual loud swallow to listen and not drown out anything. All life seemed suspended at that moment.

"The one who died in the war - the Crimean War, I mean." The monk dusted some crumbs off the table and into his hand as he spoke. "Close as brothers they all were. They're all cousins, were all cousins I should say."

"Who?" Mitchell's breath was coming in shallow bursts.

"Dominick Killelea, Michael Fegarty and the one who died." Mitchell and Maddy exchanged astonished glances.

"I hadn't realised they were related, Killelea and Fegarty," said Mitchell.

"All had the same grandparents. All from Westport in County Mayo. They did work for us here sometimes with their uncles - all of them stonemasons - before they decided that that life wasn't exciting enough for them."

"And they took the Queen's Shilling?" Mitchell suggested.

"Exactly. Joined the famous 88th all at the same time."

"I don't suppose you know where he died? In which battle? Or was it illness?" asked Mitchell. Brother Conraitus shook his head and Mitchell had to think again.

"No idea. He wasn't shot, I know that," said the monk shrugging.

"Did one of the others tell you that for certain?" Mitchell needed facts not speculation although anything would be better than nothing. Brother Conraitus nodded before speaking.

"Killelea said that if he could ever find the person responsible, he'd be paid back in kind. Hardly likely that will happen now, is it? I said that he would have to join up again to get hold of a gun and he said guns were not involved. He sounded very bitter."

"Maybe he caught one of those horrible diseases," Maddy suggested.

"Disease killed more men that guns. Nothing unusual in that after a battle," said Mitchell quietly, trying desperately to link it all up.

"I expect if you want to know about it, you'll just have to ask them about their cousin."

"Maybe I'll do just that, Brother Conraitus. Talk about old times. In the Crimea. At Inkerman." Brother Conraitus snapped his fingers in delight as Mitchell spoke.

"That's where it happened!" The monk smiled broadly as the name came back to him. Mitchell managed to return his smile - but only just. So now he knew the 'who', and almost the 'why' and he felt he was getting there. The link with the 'how' might just come back too.

"That was a most truly satisfying breakfast, Brother Conraitus," said Mitchell. The monk had risen and was heading back to the kitchen.

"Gives a body enough strength to get through the day," the monk said. Maddy shifted in her seat, got comfortable and waited for Mitchell to speak.

"I expect my orders for the day will have changed, Mr Mitchell." Maddy was a little impatient. She knew important information when she heard it even if neither of them knew exactly what it all meant. Mitchell nodded.

"How good are you at playing the damsel in distress?"

"Hopeless." Who bothered about a skivvy in distress? What world did Mr Mitchell live in, she wondered. Her hero occasionally showed slight glimpses of being fallible.

"Then it's time you got in a bit of practice." Mitchell still had no idea why he was being targeted and no longer cared. His own death was to be the culmination. Only Major Sinclair's death stood between Mitchell and all eternity. If he could keep the major away till Fegarty and Killelea were forced into action, at least one life would be spared. If Major Sinclair was not here, perhaps they would cut their losses and go straight for Mitchell himself.

"I won't do it." Maddy was adamant for she had realised what thoughts were going through Mitchell's brain.

"Then you're off the team and you owe me the price of that dinner at the Black Swan Inn in The Grassmarket while we waited for the stagecoach."

"Lady Askaig would have wanted me to be fed," she retorted defiantly.

"Not on roast beef and treacle pudding, she wouldn't. Boiled mutton, potatoes and a glass of milk would have sufficed. You owe me the difference." Maddy glowered at the table.

"It's the major you want me to meet, don't you? I've got ears too, Mr Mitchell, and a brain. Keep him away. Men always like to act like heroes," she said scornfully. "Was that what happened at Inkerman? You stole somebody's glory?" Maddy's anxiety had made her a little too bold and she knew it. "Sorry, so sorry, Mr Mitchell, but I really want to help you. I want to be here to do that." Mitchell sighed.

"It's all right, Maddy. The problem is I don't know what I did but the major might. Unfortunately he will remember too late. This engagement has been brewing for fifteen years and the major and I have the most disadvantageous position for the coming battle. You and I must now keep him out of it for in this instance, a lone campaign is the one most likely to succeed."

"You could leave with me," she suggested hopefully.

"That would only postpone the inevitable and I would have lost any slight momentary advantage I might now have."

"Which is?"

"I now know who is definitely involved. Not absolutely why it is all happening but that is not the most important part right now. Killelea and Fegarty."

"And Mrs Campbell," Maddy added astutely.

"And Mrs Campbell. Perhaps but we don't know for certain." Margaret Campbell had been there as had her sister.

"But you will bear her in mind?" He nodded. "I don't like leaving you on your own, Mr Mitchell."

"I've got Jude. He can be put on full alert. He can keep an eye on Killelea while I watch Fegarty. They won't suspect him."

"And Mrs Campbell?" Maddy suggested. But Mitchell shook his head.

"Right now she has her hands full with Lucy. That girl's on the verge of a breakdown."

"And her other aunt couldn't care less. Miss Cowan, I mean." That cut Mitchell to the quick for he knew Maddy was right.

"I think she cares in a very sterile sort of way. She's just been so ingrained with the idea that her employer's needs come before everything else that she's completely unable to act or react in any independent way. It's the way she was raised. She's not like you, Maddy. Miss Cowan is very predictable."

"And boring." Maddy was turning the knife.

"Now we can't say that for we have never met her socially." Love and lust still lingered equally in Mitchell's breast where Eliza Cowan was concerned. "Now to business. Major Sinclair is doing what he does best right now. He's on the march as we speak. He is definitely not boring but he is predictable in a very unpredictable sort of way. He'll have to stick roughly to the roads for the fields are almost impassable to a man on foot due to the drifting snow piled high over most of them. A man, a determined one, could make it here by sticking to the road if the weather holds. He would know he had a firm surface beneath the snow unlike over the fields. That man is Major Sinclair. I want you to stick to the same route, that is the edge of the road, and you will almost certainly meet up with him. Pretend to be having trouble with the ankle, tell him you're from Lord Askaig's household, smile at him a lot and he'll stay with you till you say you might just be able to make it to West Linton with his help. He knows the dead are going nowhere. Under no circumstances are you to let him know what is going on here." He had a sudden mental picture of her in her old boots.

"I'm going to buy a sturdy pair of boots with my first pay from the Agency." She was still reading his thoughts. Was she telling him he had better live long enough to pay her?

"Now that's a good idea. Get Major Sinclair to take you back into West Linton and buy a pair there. The major has all the time in the world till he buries his brother. Once in West Linton, book in at the Regent Moray. The monks are coming back here at some point so that should free up some rooms." He quickly took a gold sovereign from his pocket and handed it to her. "Stay there until I come for you." Maddy stood up suitably chastened and slipped the sovereign into her pocket.

"They'll think I've stolen it."

"No they won't," said her employer. "Tell them who you are and that you've just had an operation of sorts on your ankle. Your boot no longer fits and the housekeeper gave you money for new boots. It will come out of your wages, she says."

"So I buy new boots while you get killed?" At least she'd spared him the 'passing over' ritual.

"That's not exactly the plan. Somebody might, in fact somebody probably will get killed, but I'll make sure it's not the head of The Mitchell Detective Agency or indeed any employee of said agency. That reassure you?"

"No, Mr Mitchell. You lost your memory when your head was blown up at Inkerman."

"It was not blown up and definitely not blown off at Inkerman, Maddy. It was just somewhat rattled about a bit."

"And sliced open." Maddy had been listening to backstairs gossip.

"Just a bit. But what has that to do with my ability to stay alive?"

"Everything. You think all of this has to do with that battle but you can't actually remember what happened. What if your memory of that day comes back and it's all so horrible you freeze and they kill you?"

"I'll make sure Jude's there to poke me into action. Now, who is running this business, Miss Pearson? Get your coat on and go. Tell Major Sinclair you're going crazy amongst all these monks and are trying to get to West Linton. Just keep off the real doings here at the Priory. Major Sinclair is a very gallant and brave man whose men are devoted to him and his eccentric ways and now his life is in your hands. I know him, like him and I'm putting my finest operative on his case. Now, Maddy, enjoy the Regent Moray and buy serviceable boots."

He deliberately cut another slice of bread the moment she left the room.

"Finished?" Brother Conraitus looked in from the kitchen as Mitchell's chair scraped against the flagstones.

"I'm in your debt, Brother Conraitus,. Miss Pearson has gone on an errand for me. Right now, I had better pay my respects once more to Sir Ian and Captain Brogan."

"Brother Walter is worried about Lady Grant." The monk shook his head slowly as he spoke. "I told him that Miss Cowan will help her through it. And her son, of course," the monk added as an afterthought.

"By the way," said Mitchell, "do you remember the name of that cousin of Fegarty's? The one who died?"

"No recollection of the surname. Killelea or Fegarty probably. Which one I don't recall. His Christian name was Timothy, that I do remember." Mitchell could not remember anyone of that name but there were so many blanks.

"Well I'll leave and let you get on with your creative cooking." With that, Mitchell left the warmth and safety of the parlour fire and sampled yet again the cold, bitter air of the cloisters.

Mitchell hoped Maddy would have wrapped up well. She would no doubt have borrowed a blanket from her room to use as a shawl, with or without the Priory's permission. What Mitchell had to do right then was to force a showdown, make them act before they were completely ready and the best way to do that was to complete the plan he had set in motion when he had sent Maddy away. He knew he had it within his power to force the 'when'. But that meant passing the time of day with an erstwhile, occasional comrade, Mr Michael Fegarty. Killelea was still in Jude's sight, he hoped, and he would be so focused on revenge, he would pay little attention to a monk as ham-fisted as Brother Jude. But where exactly was Michael Fegarty?

Chapter 9

Mitchell walked quietly along the arcaded cloisters. Time to begin the charade for he was not absolutely certain that Alan Sinclair would not simply tuck Maddy under his arm and carry her to the nearest safe haven - the Priory. Time was of the essence. Two things Mitchell wanted to do. Firstly, he had to spread the rumour that Maddy had decided to make her own way home after an argument with Mitchell and secondly, he had to speak to Eliza Cowan. One of those Cowan women was involved and he still wanted to know what it was all about.

"A problem, Duncan? You looked worried." Brother Walter was everywhere, his practised eye missing nothing.

"It's the girl, Maddy Pearson, Lord Askaig's skivvy. She's decided to see herself off to West Linton and civilisation as she calls it. Bolted when my back was turned. Well, to be truthful, we had disciplinary words and now she's hopped it. My job will be on the line if she comes to any harm while I'm supposed to be in charge of her welfare."

"She'll never make it," said Brother Walter with alarm.

"Maddy's very resilient but I'll go after her just the same. But first I'll let her find out, sample so to speak, the error of her ways for a bit. Take my time getting to her."

"Looking after the welfare of a young girl of that age is too much to ask of any man. They're so emotional." The monk had probably heard enough horror stories of nuns in his day to make him glad he wasn't Lord Askaig's butler right then.

"It won't be for long now. Mrs Brady, our cook, will take her in hand once we're back at Crosteegan. How's Joe Petherbridge? Any improvement?" asked Mitchell.

"A tiny bit but even that is significant. Still in lots of pain but alive. Brother Max is watching him very closely in case there's a change one way or another." That at least reassured Mitchell that no further attempt would take place on Petherbridge's life in the near future. "Lady Grant is beginning to kill the joyous Christmas feeling round here, Duncan."

"Well, we'll all be leaving the minute it's safe to do so, Brother Walter," Mitchell assured him.

"You'll need another coachman before you can leave."

"Brother Jude might volunteer. He was brought up on an Eddelston farm and on the Crosteegan estate. He knows how to handle horses," said Mitchell.

"Right then, Duncan, I'll be on my way. Wrap up warmly."

Mitchell slipped into the echoing church and walked quickly along the nave. He resisted the temptation to linger by the red-flamed braziers and finally stopped at the Lady Chapel. But only Lady Grant and the ever-present monks were there, on their knees as usual before the coffins of the two military men. He was puzzled. Lady Grant minus the ever-present Eliza? Mitchell sat down and gave his thoughts over to dwelling on the death of Captain Brogan. If Mitchell was correct in thinking Collinge Woods Priory had been the preferred destination for his own doomsday scenario, all along, then Brogan's death had been no accident. The captain had simply been used as bait to lure Major Sinclair there. Someone was totally consumed with hatred. He looked up and from the recesses on the other side of the shadowed church, he saw that Margaret Campbell was watching him, smiling the smile that had so reassured him and all the other men she had nursed in those hellish days on the battlefield and in the hospital in Scutari. His eyes followed her as she bent down and helped Lucy to her feet. Snowdrops for the fallen. The girl had placed a small nosegay of them beside an ancient tomb. Margaret Campbell lifted the pathetic little bunch and placed it against the soaring outer wall. Everything tidy, nothing that a pious monk could slip on. The nurse was always to the fore, it seemed. Poor child, he thought as he watched the fragile Lucy leave the church with her aunt. Although there was a vast army of servants at Crosteegan, Maddy's life was still hard physically but there was a comradeship and warmth of feeling and laughter at Crosteegan. Lucy Cowan had one aunt more like a jailer and the other one completely uninterested. He rose and silently made his way towards the cloister. Word would have spread by that time that Mitchell intended leaving the Priory, to find Maddy and then probably to carry on to West Linton, intending to delegate his duty to the Grants to Major Sinclair. His prime responsibility had always been to see one of Lord Askaig's servants safely home to Crosteegan.

The bitter air hit him fractionally before the pole-axing blow and his knees buckled beneath him. The murderous look in Killelea's eyes as Mitchell twisted and went down was wiped off almost immediately as Margaret Campbell hit Killelea hard across the face. Fegarty pushed him away roughly before dragging the semi-conscious butler back into the church.

"Not out there, you fool!" Margaret Campbell's voice was no longer soft and reassuring.

"Do you think he's guessed?" Margaret Campbell nodded at Killelea.

"Yes," she said, "he knows, he knows it all now."

"What happened?" Mitchell felt himself being hauled roughly to his feet. "A little more care, Brother Jude, please." He glared at the young monk.

"You backed into a ladder, Mr Mitchell," explained Jude in a voice that told Mitchell all he wanted to know. No need to guess roughly who had been carrying the ladder.

"It's the kitchen parlour for you, Duncan," said Brother Walter. "You really should watch where you're going. Too many business deals cluttering up that head of yours. If Mr Fegarty hadn't hauled you away in the nick of time, your head would have hit the pillar there and you'd have eaten your last hearty breakfast. As it is, it's no more than a few bruises." So that was the yarn they were spinning.

"My eternal gratitude, Michael," said Mitchell as he shuffled slowly along to the kitchen parlour, the backs of his legs feeling as if they had splintered.

"The ladder smashed into the back of your knees. Mr Killelea had just come down from removing some snow from the roof that would have badly hurt anyone beneath it if it had collapsed on him. You backed into the ladder as he was coming along the cloister carrying it." Once more Brother Jude's voice cut through the pain that was searing its own path through Mitchell's consciousness and their eyes met as Mitchell eased himself in agony into Brother Conraitus's own cushioned chair by the kitchen parlour fire. Mitchell received the warning loud and clear despite the pain that was now slowing him down.

"Brother Jude shouted a warning but it was too late. He ran to help from the other side of the cloister," Brother Walter explained.

"Mrs Campbell appeared and helped you, Mr Mitchell." Jude's eyes held so many messages of warning that Mitchell in his state of mental confusion was hard-pressed to answer. Reassurance and direction were urgently needed by the young rebel. But that was exactly what he was, young and untried. Mitchell now accepted the fact that he needed an old hand and he knew where to find him.

"Brother Jude?" Mitchell's head was buzzing, the sounds from the kitchen blotting out all efforts by his befuddled brain to cut through the mundane and eliminate the peripheral messages to get to the cold logic that would keep him alive. "Brother Jude?" he repeated and hoped the boy had not decided he had been mistaken.

"I'm here, Mr Mitchell." Jude's face swam into view as the cowled head looked him straight in the eye yet again.

"Thank you for your quick response." Their eyes locked and the young man waited for his orders.

"I'm to sit with you until you've recovered, Mr Mitchell. Brother Walter's orders. Just you and me against the world of culinary experts." They both smiled and Mitchell got the message. They were more or less alone in the kitchen parlour, the monks still cooking frantically in the huge kitchen next door for any clerical visitors who happened by during the Christmas season. Their culinary expertise was well-known and visitors were plentiful especially at that time. Fegarty, Killelea and Margaret Campbell were elsewhere and Jude had sussed out that that was the direction from which the danger would emanate for Mitchell. But Jude's help was not the help that was required most. An old head was needed and Mitchell was not up to it right then. Nor was his body for that original blow to his head had slowed him down alarmingly. A few hour's rest by the fire would help but those hours were a luxury he could not afford. A drastic change in plans was now called for. But he could only do so much and the other two were mere children in terms of hard-bitten experience. Hard-bitten experience of the best kind was in the vicinity and Mitchell had just made sure it left. God Almighty! Maddy had been delegated to lead Major Sinclair out of the danger zone. Now Jude was about to be ordered to bring him back. Alan Sinclair was wily, fair and hopelessly eccentric but also mean, vicious and inventive in a tight corner and those were qualities Mitchell desperately needed right then. He brushed aside any regrets of having to rethink his plans for the major's safety. They were only postponing the inevitable anyway if Mitchell failed at the Priory. The puzzle was why Margaret Campbell had stopped the others from finishing the job. He would worry about that later always assuming there would be a 'later'.

"Do you think your head will clear up soon, Mr Mitchell?" Jude was no fool. He had almost certainly witnessed it all as he had been following Killelea and knew time was of the essence. It was to the boy's credit that he had not backed off. He had been wise enough to realise that his story of what had taken place set against the other three's collective version of what had happened to Mitchell would not only have been denied by them, but also he would have been marked down as a potential victim of yet another accident once he had left the Priory. Mitchell wondered yet again how they could think him capable of an action so mean that they would wait fifteen years for revenge.

"Jude?"

"Right here, Mr Mitchell."

"You're going on a journey."

"Fortune-telling now, is it? A long journey? I think Mr Mitchell's head has been in contact with the spirits, Mrs Campbell." So Margaret Campbell had reappeared.

"How is he, Brother Jude?"

"Personally, I think he's here for another few hours. That blow to his legs and ribs on top of the one he received in Edinburgh has slowed him down to a snail's pace physically and he's none too clever mentally either."

"But surely he's mentally aware, brother?" Margaret Campbell wanted Mitchell to experience and understand everything. Her distress was obvious but not misunderstood by the young, erratic monk.

"Oh yes, nothing to worry about, nothing a few hours' rest won't put right. I know of nothing that can stop Mr Mitchell accomplishing what he sets out to do. Known him for donkey's years. I grew up in Eddleston and my father and his brothers all worked on the Crosteegan estate."

"Not even brick walls, Brother Jude? Would one of those not stop him?" she suggested.

"He'd just climb right over it."

"That, Brother Jude, is not always the best move." The bitterness was there now in Margaret Campbell's voice.

"Well, Mrs Campbell, he won't be making a move of any kind for some time. I've been delegated to watch over him by Brother Walter himself who probably got them from Father Prior."

"I can see he is in good hands," said Margaret Campbell, her voice having recovered its sympathetic tones.

"The best, I can assure you. He will not be left alone for a moment. Our Prior said it would be more than his life was worth to let anything happen to Crosteegan's butler. Lady Askaig would have his head and Lord Askaig would never set foot within these walls again. The reputation of Collinge Woods Priory would be ruined at a stroke and loads of revenue lost into the bargain."

"Then I shall leave you to it, Brother Jude. Perhaps, when he is feeling better, he would join us in the Lady Chapel. I'm sure Lady Grant would wish to be reassured of his recovery from his own lips."

"As he seems to be dozing now, I'll be sure to tell him when he revives a little, Mrs Campbell." With that Margaret Campbell left the parlour as quietly as she had entered it. "She seems anxious, Mr Mitchell, for you to meet her in the church," Jude whispered.

"I wonder why?" said Mitchell. "I have a task for you, Jude."

"I don't think you should be on your own."

"Nor do I but right now I'm quite safe and if you can accomplish this with all haste, I won't be on my own for long. I think they want me in a specific place, not here. God only knows why. I've sent Maddy to meet Major Sinclair and keep him away from here. Now trust me, Jude. Don't ask the ins and outs, just listen. Change of plan. I want you to track them down, Maddy and Major Sinclair. Tell him old scores from the Battle of Inkerman are being settled, that he and I are the targets and the enemy is here in the Priory. There are three of them, two men and one woman. He's to decide what his own response to that is. I'd like him to be here but it's up to him. It has already begun and his brother, Captain Brogan's death was to be the bait used to lure him here. Whether Captain Brogan's actual death had nothing to do with them, was perhaps the result of natural causes, is not important. He was destined to have at least an accident in order to bring Major Sinclair here. Now, Jude, get moving, for we've no time to lose."

"I'm here. I could help," Jude protested.

"Old heads are needed, Jude, old, cynical and very experienced ones. This is an eye for an eye and all those bible stories haven't prepared you for this. This is not the Garden of Eden. There's more than one snake here." Mitchell slumped back in the chair as the pain flashed like lightning through his befuddled brain.

"You should move into the kitchen itself, Mr Mitchell, and Brother Conraitus would look after you."

"I'll be alright. Keep out of sight as you leave the Priory and they'll believe you're still here. Now go and deliver the message to Major Sinclair but keep Maddy well away. They should be on the road to West Linton. If Major Sinclair decides to come here, don't let her follow him. Either keep her where she is till somebody comes for the two of you or take her on to West Linton. Tell her that's an order I've given both of you."

"I'm on my way, Mr Mitchell." Mitchell nodded and closed his eyes as the monk left to meet up with Maddy.

Mitchell had been invited by Margaret Campbell to meet him in the church and he would be a fool to go. That was where she wanted him to be, that place had some sort of significance in all of this. But Sinclair would come, he was certain of that. He'd give him an hour or so to get to the Priory and then reassess the situation. Another hour would see himself rested and recovered - he hoped. What had he done that day at Inkerman to set all this in motion? What had he and the major done? But why had those three waited for fifteen years? And why was Margaret Campbell involved? Mitchell's mind simply could not rest. One of him and three of them with Margaret Campbell's cool, calculating mind plotting, manipulating, manoeuvring, taking an insane pleasure in turning the screw. She knew he suspected, had even led him along the trail of thought required to fulfil her plan. But she had only told him so much, just enough to let him know that flight was not an option. Retribution would always be waiting sometime, somewhere in the wings. He shivered in spite of the warmth emanating from the flame-filled fireplace.

"A good plate of soup, Mr Mitchell. That's what's needed. I'm sure Mrs Brady would agree." Brother Conraitus placed an empty bowl and spoon on the well-scrubbed table. Mitchell had the distinct feeling he would throw up the lot.

"In a little while, Brother Conraitus, that would be perfect. Ate a little too much of your delicious cheese at breakfast and the taste is still lingering."

"My soup's pretty delicate today. Not a hearty broth but cream of celery. But maybe you'd best wait a while right enough."

Mitchell woke with a start. He had dozed off and wondered if it had been for minutes or hours. Not hours, he told himself, for either Sinclair or Jude would have appeared by now. He felt a lot better, not great but at least human. The kitchen sounds were more muted. A long, cool drink would have been wonderful. When this was all over, he intended sitting by the fire in his own room at Crosteegan with a generous glass of port and a good book. He yearned for the normality of Crosteegan.

"Ready for something to eat now, Mr Mitchell?" Brother Conraitus had bustled in and oddly enough, Mitchell suddenly felt hungry.

"Soup, bread and cheese would be perfect if it's not too much trouble."

"No problem." They were quickly set before him accompanied by a pot of refreshing ale, not spiced. Mitchell did it all justice to the monk's obvious satisfaction.

"I think I must have slept for a bit."

"That you did and missed all the excitement." Mitchell was on full alert.

"What happened? Nothing serious, I hope," he added before the brother could answer.

"Missing person."

"Who?" Jude? he wondered.

"Miss Lucy Cowan." Mitchell relaxed.

"She's probably just wandered off but in this weather that could prove fatal when a girl is so." Mitchell's voice tailed off. How did one describe Lucy Cowan?

"Unworldly." Brother Conraitus finished the sentence for him.

"I suppose so," Mitchell agreed. "She seems to lack a certain appreciation of the dangers present in everyday living." Mitchell was rambling for something was beginning to make his stomach muscles tighten, some sort of intuitive alarm was rising in him. Was this the beginning of the end?

"She's a very vulnerable girl. Her aunt is completely distraught," said the monk.

"They're still looking for her? Inside the Priory? Surely she didn't wander outside?" said Mitchell.

"That's where they found her." Mitchell relaxed a little at this information.

"So she's safe and well?"

"Yes, well, safe anyway. The rest is in the lap of the gods. Sorry, God, I should have said, Mr Mitchell." Brother Conraitus smiled weakly.

"What exactly is her state of health?" asked Mitchell anxiously. The monk sighed and stopped tidying up.

"They found her lying in the snow just by the outer Priory wall. Badly beaten about the head and buried in the snow. Luckily one of the brothers spotted a piece of cloth - part of her jacket, it seems, sticking out, dark against the white snow."

"You said buried." The monk nodded, his face serious and frowning.

"That's the word used by Brother Walter. I didn't see the girl myself."

"But she's still alive?" The monk nodded and stopped rearranging his desk.

"They didn't think so at first and the aunt ran off before they managed to revive the girl in the infirmary. Lucy's managing to pull round slowly but she's very ill from the physical attack on her and her time in the freezing snow. Brother Max is quite hopeful of a complete recovery - eventually."

"But buried. That sounds like a deliberate act. The outer wall will not shed any heavy snowfall. It's too narrow at the top to support any amount of snow."

"Yes." That one word conveyed the general conclusion of all involved, it seemed. Simple confirmation. Mitchell's mind was furiously trying to understand it and also where he himself came into it for it had certainly exploded all his theories and plans. The girl was going to recover. Brother Max was a prophet of doom and if he was hopeful then they could all relax as far as Lucy's immediate health was concerned. But who would want to kill Lucy? She was already in a very weak emotional state and it now seemed that Margaret Campbell was the one most concerned with her welfare as always. Margaret Campbell was an enigma. But had she suddenly turned on Lucy? Or had the two men decided that Lucy had learned something and could not be relied on to keep silent?

"And Mrs Campbell thinks her niece is dead?" he said.

"No, but she's opted to sit by herself in the Lady Chapel and leave the nursing to Brother Max and his helpers. Odd for I do believe she herself was a nurse once."

"She was and an excellent one at that." Memories flashed through Mitchell's mind's eye and this time he made no attempt to erase them. He let the scenes come and go, his stomach tied in agonising knots, his muscles aching with tension. The wall, climbing it, Eliza caught up in it, the 88th, Major Sinclair beside him. All revealed, stark and startling but still an elusive mystery. They had to go over the wall. It had stood blocking their advance. The major's orders. Mitchell's orders. All passed down the ranks. They had begun to advance, to climb that wall. The explosion, Scutari and that was it.

"So Mrs Campbell left the infirmary for the Lady Chapel?" It was still going on. Nothing had changed.

"Brother Max was surprised and he told her he thought another female should be present with the girl. She told him to get Maddy."

"Maddy's gone to West Linton."

"Mrs Campbell didn't want to hear anything. She just left as has Jude, I see," the monk remarked sourly.

"Gone on an errand for me, I'm afraid. But I thought you said that her aunt had run off thinking the girl was dead."

"She did. The other aunt, Miss Cowan. She was out there helping to search for Lucy - was absolutely frantic. As I said before, when they found the girl, she looked dead, no question about it. We were all agreed on that and Miss Cowan ran away. Just took off out of the gate."

"So she still thinks that Lucy is dead.?" asked Mitchell dazed by what he had just heard.

"Probably unless she's returned to the Priory. Father Prior said to give her half an hour to calm down, to reappear, and then if she hasn't, to go after her."

"Was she dressed for walking outside?" Mitchell's anxiety was deepening. Brother Contraitus just shrugged.

"Dressed for the freezing cold of the Lady Chapel, no doubt. It's more or less the same thing." Brother Conraitus spoke from long experience.

"So Eliza Cowan has finally left Lady Grant's side," said Mitchell.

"Seems like it."

"So Mrs Campbell has now taken her place beside Lady Grant?" asked Mitchell.

"Not so, Mr Mitchell, for I noticed at the service that Mrs Campbell was sitting alone there apart from two monks." Mitchell's heart sank. Margaret Campbell, Fegarty and Killelea. All together, all waiting for him.

"So where is Lady Grant?" Brother Conraitus shook his head. Mitchell frowned. So Lady Grant was missing too, it seemed. Well, at least from her usual haunt. And the cold-blooded Eliza frantic with dread and grief and filled with what? Revenge! That was what the Cowan women did best, it seemed. But why Eliza for Lucy and not the girl's mother? Hell's teeth! Another mystery solved! Eliza and Lucy, mother and daughter. But why had Eliza always been glued to Lady Grant? Margaret Campbell had left Lucy but she had not harmed her in any way. She was so eaten up now by making sure her time to right a wrong had come that nothing and no-one would be in her mind but that. Mitchell suddenly leapt to his feet.

"Are you ill, Mr Mitchell?"

"Which way did Miss Cowan go?"

"I don't know. Just hared off out of the main gate. After that, I've no idea." Brother Conraitus shook his head. "She'll be back. The brothers are still keeping a watch of sorts. She's only been gone a short time." Mitchell's brain was rapidly processing it all. If she were lost out there, or worse still if she accomplished what he thought she'd set out to do, she could be as good as dead whichever way you looked at it. Which way to go? He had to get it right. And if he did not? He refused to face that scenario.

Chapter 10

Mitchell's race finished abruptly at the main gate of the Priory. He stopped dead at the sight. The pristine snow of the surrounding grounds had been trashed to slush by the monks searching for Lucy. Eliza's footprints would only be recognised much farther away. But which way was he to go? He opted for the obvious, the avenue of elms leading down to the long drive and then to the main road, then changed his mind. He had to get into the mindset of the person responsible for attacking Lucy. The obvious could be tackled later. He would know if he were wrong soon enough for the fields would show up any small footprints recently made - or none. His eyes hurt, blinded almost by the constant scanning of the painfully white mass surrounding him. Then he saw them, further away, well beyond the Priory walls. Two sets of footprints carelessly made as each of the women had stumbled her way through the deep snow, one following the other. Mitchell cut across the field dragging himself after them, his eyes still looking for their moving figures ahead. The fields about were open and yet locked in winter's icy grip, they seemed to suffocate him. He looked desperately for a break in the never-ending blanket of snow and found it about a quarter of-a-mile ahead and off to his right. He hoped Brother Walter and the others were following. A small copse was what it was, its trees bent low under the weight of the snow. His heart dreaded what he would find there.

"Eliza! Don't do it! Please do not do this." His voice echoed loudly in his ears, sharp even in the still, frosty air. He stopped atop the bank of a broad, deep ditch, its sloping side dropping steeply down to the frozen bed beneath it. "Don't, please don't." His tone this time had lost its edge. He now had himself more under control. But she did not for one second respond to the concern for her in his plea. She stood one foot almost in the stagnant, shattered, ice-topped water, the other firmly on the bank, Lady Grant lying prone at her feet, her hair firmly in Eliza's grasp.

"Leave her. The price is too great. Leave her and let the law deal with her." Eliza's right hand tugged sharply on the hair, pulling the head right back, her other one digging deep into Lady Grant's shoulder. "Leave her alone, Eliza. Go back to Lucy."

"Lucy's dead." Eliza Cowan sounded dead too.

"No she isn't." Eliza Cowan shook her head and tugged Lady Grant's head back yet again. Mitchell began to make his way down but stopped abruptly as Eliza looked up, her face drawn and pale, her own hair completely dishevelled. No bonnet, no coat. Red hair fell to her shoulders, glossy and a mass of unruly curls. She must have been expecting Lady Grant to be resting. "Don't you come near," she warned. Mitchell slithered to a halt. " This is evil I'm holding in my hands."

"I know that," he said softly. "Let me take her back to the Priory and she can tell everything to the authorities when they question her. They'll come straight away from West Linton." Mitchell moved slowly, slid softly further down the slope.

"Why are you moving , Mr Mitchell?" She spoke almost casually and that alarmed Mitchell even more.

"Eliza, you know why. I don't want you to do this. I don't want you to waste your life." Mitchell did not give one damn for Lady Grant. Perhaps he should have out of common decency but he did not. He knew now who had wielded that knife upon Lucy's wrists. Twice she had tried to kill Lucy Cowan and had he been in Eliza's place, he would have finished her off after the first attempt. "Eliza, Lucy needs you. I give you my word that Brother Max expects her to recover. She's already regained consciousness," Mitchell pleaded and knew he was wasting his time. The only thing that would succeed would be force. How long did it take to drown an unconscious person, he wondered, for he was sure that was what Eliza intended doing. There was still a chance if he rushed Eliza before she managed to plunge the woman yet again into the ice-filled ditch. "Don't drown her. There are other ways of making her pay."

"Are you suggesting I just walk away and leave her like this, Mr Mitchell?"

"Other ways, Eliza, lawful ways that will allow you to be with Lucy."

"When did I become Eliza in your mind?" The sudden switch threw him for a moment.

"Ten years ago. I see I have never been Duncan in yours." His eyes drifted to her hands as he spoke but they had not released their strong grip on her potential victim. Mitchell became edgy as the seconds ticked by and the unconscious woman lay in the freezing wet of the slush and sharp ice-shards now scattered about on the surface of the water and its banks. Suddenly Eliza Cowan looked away from Mitchell and grabbed the other woman's shoulders. But Mitchell moved swiftly and pushed her roughly aside. Lady Grant could roast in hell but she was not taking Eliza Cowan with her if Mitchell could help it. Eliza staggered back and fell into the sluggish, chilling water. He stepped in quickly and hauled her out again. She shook herself free of him immediately. Mitchell looked slowly from Lady Grant to Eliza Cowan's deathly pale face.

"Why didn't you tell me?" he said after a pain-filled silence between them. He looked long and hard once more at the corpse of Sir Ian's widow, his stomach heaving at the sight.

"You didn't ask." Eliza Cowan sighed deeply and pushed her hair back from her pale face. "She tried twice to kill my daughter. She deserved this, she deserved to die." Mitchell forced himself to look again.

"But a lethal shard of ice beat you to it when she fell into the ditch." He could see the fatal, arrow-like piece protruding from the jugular, the blood now seeping up through the ice and slush in the water. He wondered briefly what were the emotions that had passed through Eliza Cowan's brain as she realised that, in her desperation to escape, Lady Grant had caused her own death. Was he relieved or sad that a life had ended thus? He would never really know for Brother Walter and some of his monks loomed up on top of the ditch just then and interrupted his thoughts. He watched as they slipped and slithered their way down to the bottom.

"Followed your footsteps, Duncan." Brother Walter's voice faded quickly to almost nothing. Mitchell pointed to the shard. One of the younger monks was violently and noisily sick.

"Dead, I'm afraid. She fell into the ice-covered ditch. Miss Cowan tried to pull her out and I had to rescue the would-be rescuer as you can see. The entire area is icy and slippery."

"What a dreadful accident. Exactly the same thing happened to one of the brothers last week. It was his arm that was almost severed. He has been very fortunate to survive. What will Father Prior think?" They both knew what Father Prior would think - yet another occupant for the Lady Chapel. "Best get Lady Grant's remains back to the Priory. We brought a stretcher just in case there had been an accident. Are you alright, Miss Cowan?" Eliza nodded to the monk and accepted the blanket he offered her.

"Thank you, Brother Walter. I'll walk back slowly if you don't mind. How is Lucy?"

"Recovering, I'm told. Badly beaten about the head but perfectly lucid now. You'll see that Miss Cowan gets back safely, Duncan? And is not out in this chill air any longer than is wise?" Mitchell nodded and watched them go, their sorry bundle carried easily by the monks.

Eliza made no effort to follow on behind the stretcher. She brushed the snow from a fallen tree trunk and sank down slowly, her eyes firmly on the horizon. Mitchell could almost feel the intense fatigue emanating from her. She was feeling cheated, feeling she had let Lucy down and Mitchell understood that.

"I should have done something to sort this out the first time. I should have made Lucy feel safe forever."

"Lucy's safe now and I doubt if anything you did could have stopped the woman from." Mitchell's voice faltered.

"Yes, you're right, Mr Mitchell, she is safe but only after having had to live through two dreadful experiences because of me. What kind of mother does that make me?"

"A caring one. You care for her. You love her. You worked to keep her." Eliza Cowan shook her head firmly.

"There was no problem with money. Her father always saw to that."

"Sir Ian?" There was only a fraction's hesitation before she answered.

"Yes. He called her Robin, his pet name for her because she seemed to him to be such a fragile little bird."

"Then they met?" asked Mitchell.

"As frequently as he could manage. Many times a year. He doted on her and now she's lost him and is fragile to the point of breaking. Lady Grant told Lucy last night she had killed him by coming to Edinburgh from Lasswade. She has been brought up by my parents who live there. Lady Grant said he'd died of shame."

"Who killed Cock Robin? Lucy told Maddy she had killed Robin."

"She thought her image in Sir Ian's mind had died and she had been the cause of that. Robin died when Lady Grant filled Lucy's mind with her poisonous insinuations. Lucy's life has been too sheltered, too protected."

"So Lady Grant knew Sir Ian had a daughter by you?" Eliza Cowan nodded.

"It happened when I'd gone home after that explosion. He visited me and there was a very brief - liason." She paused and Mitchell waited patiently for her to continue.

"Lady Grant knew everything. She always knew everything about everybody. I stayed with her when she pleaded with me to do so because I felt I owed her it. I had betrayed her friendship and I felt guilty, always guilty, a lifetime of guilt. Lucy stayed with my parents in Lasswade most of the time."

"Who told Lady Grant about Lucy?"

"I never asked but it wasn't Sir Ian. She never even mentioned it. One brief moment together and it has ended like this."

"And Margaret was delegated to look after Lucy until you met up with Roderick Grant?"

"Yes, but it seems she left her alone this morning and Lady Grant slipped away from me. I'd stuck with Lady Grant night and day after the first incident."

"So Lady Grant tried to slit Lucy's wrists?" said Mitchell. Eliza Cowan nodded.

"I thought I would wait till after the funeral before I would figure out what was to be done to keep Lucy safe."

"Do you think it was grief at Sir Ian's death that turned Lady Grant's mind to killing. I must say that it sounds like a pretty drastic reaction to me." Mitchell sat down beside her.

"Her fury was basically at Sir Ian." The light began to dawn for Mitchell.

"So she was the one responsible for damaging the coffin." Eliza nodded.

"I discovered her doing it and dragged her away. Lucy witnessed it."

"But why was she so angry after all these years?" Eliza sighed deeply.

"I think now she has always harboured a hatred for Lucy and me but it was Sir Ian's will that turned that hatred into action. She discovered the contents of his will when he died. Captain Brogan gave her two envelopes both addressed to Sir Ian he had collected from Sir Ian's club."

"And one was a lovely Christmas card from Lucy? From Robin?" Eliza nodded.

"It was the same kind of card every year. Always unsigned for there was always a robin in it somewhere. She drew it in herself. It was their little bit of fun."

"And so the other envelope contained the will that I suppose sent Lady Grant on her murderous rampage?" Mitchell suggested.

"Yes." Eliza Cowan agreed. "I already knew the contents of the will. Sir Ian had told me many years before. Sir Ian left the house in Eddleston to me. He assumed Lucy would live with me if she had not married by that time. Everything else including the house in London went to Lucy but with life-rent of that house allowed to Lady Grant. There was a small annuity to go with it for her. Roderick has an excellent job with the government but Sir Ian was anxious that his daughter - he acknowledged her as such on her birth certificate here in Scotland - that Lucy would be financially independent. He loved her. They were constantly in touch." The birth certificate had probably been the means that enlightened Lady Grant, a lady who had always wanted to know everything about everybody, it seemed.

"So Lucy's grieving for a beloved father," said Mitchell.

"Or being prevented from doing so until now." She stood up abruptly and began the long trek back to the Priory.

"You said Lady Grant knew everything."

"She made a point of it. She just liked knowing. I'm sure she never used any of the information she collected. That was not her way."

"Did she know your sister's husband?"

"Timothy Campbell? Yes, she did." So that was it. Timothy, the monk had said. Timothy Campbell. They could see the Priory looming starkly against an azure blue sky.

"How did that come about?" asked Mitchell.

"He worked on the house in Eddleston. As you know, it's a former Abbot's lodge. Sir Ian was keen to keep and restore the original stonework when he had first bought it long ago. He owned it long before we moved into it because of his overseas service with the regiment."

"And Timothy Campbell was a stonemason," said Mitchell. It was all coming together. "And he eventually joined the 88th? Sir Ian's regiment?" he asked. Eliza Cowan nodded.

"Along with his cousins Dominick Killelea and Michael Fegarty. Margaret met him in Eddelston when she was visiting me. I must find her and tell her what's happened, Mr Mitchell."

"It's all right, Miss Cowan, I'll find her or rather I think she'll find me."

"Why does she want to see you?"

"There's something I think she wants to discuss with me." They had reached the main gate and she turned to him.

"Probably about the wall. She said you were there with Timothy when he died."

Chapter 11

Lady Grant had been coffined. A makeshift affair. There were obviously no women members of the community and Brother Max had been at a loss as to what to do when the body had been brought to him. But Eliza had stepped in and prepared the corpse before it was taken to the Lady Chapel where it now lay. Mitchell's professional eye had subconsciously noted that that small in-shot was now somewhat overcrowded. But the lady now lay there in state beside her husband like the kings and queens of old. A very short period of silent observance was to be held later that evening once the brothers had thawed out. Mitchell knew that he was now on his own. Alan Sinclair would have already reached the Priory if Jude had contacted him. Maddy had probably done too good a job and they were probably well on their way to West Linton by then. He could have asked Eliza to try to negotiate a peace of sorts but she had suffered enough for the moment, he thought, and besides, Margaret Campbell was now beyond reason, it seemed. A husband's death had to be avenged. There had been nothing else in her life for fifteen years - only revenge. But why now?

The Priory's inhabitants were at dinner. The winter's evening would be long, the afternoon already fading into gloom. The vast church was still, silent, in almost total darkness, the building empty but for its now eternally-silent occupants. Even the monks had abandoned their vigil for a short time to eat as they were no longer competing in the piety stakes with Lady Grant. Food first, duty second and Mitchell commended their good sense. A wise decision, he thought as he walked warily along the eastern aisle. Only small candles placed on altars and in tiny niches at irregular intervals illuminated feebly the dark recesses of the building.

"What am I looking for, Mrs Campbell?" Mitchell suddenly called out into the eerie, threatening, stillness of the ancient walls. His voice seemed to echo impotently forever. "You're my guide, aren't you, always leading me on?" The soft, sensual sound of a woman's quiet laughter tingled somewhere ahead of him.

"Yes, Mr Mitchell, we have been waiting for you - for fifteen years." Margaret Campbell's voice was quiet and totally controlled. Her time had come and she was in the mood to savour it. Then a heavy silence reigned again before Mitchell's voice shattered it.

"I know that. There's you, Michael and Dominick. You're taking Timothy's place is that right? I am right, am I not? Timothy Campbell, the third cousin?"

"You are right, Duncan. The boys of the old 88th." Fegarty this time from somewhere in the bleak shadows, moving around as he spoke. Mitchell's voice was laced with scorn when he spoke again.

"I had some good comrades in that regiment whenever I served alongside it, men of worth, men who could be relied on to stand shoulder to shoulder with their comrades when the going got rough. You weren't one of them, Michael." Mitchell spat the words out and suddenly raised his voice. "And neither were you, Dominick. A family trait, is it?" Where was Killelea? Mitchell kept moving slowly and relentlessly along the never-ending length of the aisle, further into its black depths, further away from help of any kind. Forward or back, it did not much matter for they were all about him, constantly changing places.

"Frightened?" asked Margaret Campbell, her voice low, amusement lacing her speech.

"Of what? The dark? Two deadheads?" replied Mitchell scornfully.

"Bastard!" A whip clipped his cheek and the stinging pain as he jerked his head back ripped through him. So Killelea was alongside him and to his right. Mitchell kept on going in spite of it.

"Am I getting close?" he asked again.

"To the end of it all?" asked Margaret Campbell from somewhere in that eternal darkness. "Not quite there yet. You're just going on a sightseeing tour first, that's all." The soothing tones of the nurse at Scutari. He kept moving forward. He was virtually in a dark tunnel, weakly lit occasionally by almost burned out candles for this part of the building was obviously seldom used.

"Keep moving!" Killelea was now behind him and Mitchell felt the sharp point of a blade dig momentarily into his back. They seemed to be constantly and silently moving about him, behind, alongside, in front, always changing places, always keeping him confused. Margaret Campbell was an excellent tactician. Under different circumstances, he would have admired that. No guns required. That was what Killelea had said to Jude. So what was it to be and why? Knives, they probably had. Was that how he was to die? There was definitely no help nearby. An empty church except for the recently deceased, sleeping the eternal sleep.

"Enjoying the tour?" Fegarty laughed at his own little joke. A bundle was suddenly thrust at Mitchell from out of the penetrating blackness. He caught it automatically and realised it was Lucy's small posy of winter blooms.

"Flowers instead of a wreath, is that it, Mrs Campbell?" called Mitchell, his voice echoing in the relentless stillness of the night. He kept on walking slowly forward.

"To be laid in memory of the betrayed, dear Duncan," she replied. The barely controlled fury contained in those quiet words sent shivers of fear racing down his spine. God! If only he could figure it all out. His mind alternated between wanting to know and not wanting to waste time on something that might not be guaranteed to keep him alive. But how was he to know? If only he could reason with her for he knew now that she was the controlling mind in all of this. Fegarty and Killelea were mere pawns, tools she was using to forge her revenge.

"Let's talk about this, Margaret." Killelea and Fegarty exploded with laughter, mocking Mitchell's feeble attempt to stay alive.

"Margaret, is it?" said Fegarty. "Our Timothy would not have liked that one bit. He wouldn't have liked you talking to his wife as if she was a common whore." The whip flashed once more to show Killelea's agreement and sliced along the hand holding Lucy's flowers. Mitchell managed to clutch them tightly in spite of the pain. The flat blade of a sword flashed through a splinter of moonlight and hit off Mitchell's chest. Fegarty's contribution. The breath-sapping blow caused him to stagger back and he fell heavily against the marble, table-top effigy of some long-dead cleric and onto the ice-cold floor. The only thing between Mitchell and death was their desire to keep him alive a little while longer. The tour was evidently still some distance from its final destination. A boot kicked viciously into his thigh as he lay on the ground and his leg went dead for a moment. He reached out desperately to haul himself back onto his feet, his fingers scrambling for a hold in the threatening darkness. A knife was slipped into his hand, the handle thick and comforting, the blade long, narrow and lethal. Jude? Where was he now, Mitchell wondered, for not for one second had the person emerged from the darkness engulfing everything and everybody. Jude knew! Jude understood! Sinclair would have reacted differently - shoulder to shoulder against the foe. It had to be Jude and the boy had realised that it had to be faced right then or life would be one long nightmare waiting for the axe to drop. Mitchell slipped the knife up his sleeve and hauled himself onto his feet.

"Where do you want me to lay the flowers, Mrs Campbell?" Mitchell had resumed his long walk. And suddenly he knew where he was intended to be, where all Margaret Campbell's manipulation would end. It was where she had placed the flowers earlier that day with Lucy. "It was over there, if I remember correctly, the wall opposite the first prior's tomb," he called out.

"That's right, Mr Mitchell, at the foot of the wall." Mitchell's mind froze momentarily at Margaret Campbell's words. Suddenly Duncan Mitchell was no longer in the fog that had seeped into his mind that day at Inkerman. He now remembered it all with alarming clarity. He had reached the end of the walk. He hoped fervently that Jude was still around somewhere. The cold feel of the pointed steel gave him some degree of comfort and hope.

"Here? Do you want me to place them here?" Mitchell's voice sounded strong and in control and he did not understand how he achieved that.

"Right against the wall, Mr Mitchell. You remember the wall at Inkerman, don't you?" Suddenly torches placed in sconces on each side of the wall before him burst into flames and then settled, shedding their fitful, yellow glow all around. They illuminated a colossal, marble panel set into it the wall which rose up before him, dedicated to the memory of those who had died in the Crimea. White, blue-veined marble, its glistening surface resembled falling tears. Mitchell remembered shedding a few himself in private on more than one occasion during his service with The Black Watch. He swallowed back the emotion that boiled to the surface. No time now for that. He wondered if Timothy Campbell's name was there but he could not make out the regiment commemorated in the flickering light. Had Sir Ian commissioned it?

"To our glorious dead." Fegarty's sarcastic voice echoed through the church.

"And you and Dominick here were two of them, weren't you Michael? Buried you myself. Dug deep into the icy ground till my back was nearly broken that morning. I never believed in resurrection until the last few days. What yarn have they spun you, Mrs Campbell? They're liars of the first water. What lies have they been telling you?"

"There are no lies any more, just the truth at last," Margaret Campbell replied.

"From them, Mrs Campbell? You're an intelligent woman. Surely you don't believe a word they say?"

" I believe Lady Grant." Where had Margaret Campbell been these last few hours? Plotting with Fegarty and Killelea? Mitchell raised his voice once again.

"Lady Grant is dead. She's in her coffin and lying in the Lady Chapel," he said brutally. Had Margaret Campbell not realised what had happened to Lucy?

"I'm aware of that sad fact. An accident probably caused through grief."

"Then you'll also know that Lucy was buried alive."

"And she's recovering. I asked Brother Max."

"Buried, Mrs Campbell. Are you hearing but not listening?"

"Snow falls from roofs all the time in winter."

"Lucy was buried by human hands, beaten first and buried by the lady you've put your faith in, have believed every word she and those other liars have told you. Lady Grant hated all the Cowans and you can easily figure out why. She used you. Probably used these two as well just to avenge herself on your family. When did she first suggest to you, Michael, this business of salving your conscience, a conscience troubled by abandoning your own kith and kin. One of the times when you were working at your trade in the neighbourhood of Eddleston? At The Manor? When Sir Ian was well out of the way? All this was her idea, her revenge - revenge on Sir Ian and the Cowans." A knife missed Mitchell's face by inches, only the flickering light spoiling his aim.

"Stop that!" screamed Margaret Campbell. "This is no summary execution! This is justice and he has a right to speak." The silence that followed was broken suddenly.

"I've got Killelea's knife, Mr Mitchell." Jude had emerged from the darkness and now stood resolutely by Mitchell's side, Killelea's knife in his hand.

"Still got this!" Killelea produced a bayonet with a flourish and Mitchell could feel the fear emanating from the young monk but Jude did not outwardly waver for a moment. Killelea stood poised, arrogant, bayonet in one hand, the whip in the other. But Mitchell went on relentlessly at Margaret Campbell.

"Mrs Campbell, Sir Ian left everything to Lucy and Eliza in his will and his wife was determined none of you would enjoy that legacy."

"Lady Grant was wealthy in her own right. You don't know as much as you think you do, Mr Mitchell."

"It had nothing to do with money, Mrs Campbell. It was the principle of it, the loss of face and she was a very proud woman as we both know. That will of Sir Ian's would be in the public domain eventually and there was no way she could stop it." But Killelea had heard enough.

"He's all talk, just playing for time. Well, as far as I'm concerned, his time's up. Michael, time to dole out justice." Dominick Killelea's favourite whip flashed and cracked through the still, chill air, but became entangled with the ancient, cracked stone ball perched precariously above him on the cap of the pillar almost flush with the wall. They all watched in stunned silence as the whip dragged it down and Killelea's head was reduced to minced-meat and ground bone as the solid orb crushed it beneath its massive weight. Mitchell looked on in horror as Killelea, what was left of him, staggered back and slumped slowly down the wall. A bloody mass of dripping, pulped gore sat on top of his shoulders, unrecognisable as a human head. Jude threw up and sank to his knees, his hand, though, still gripping Killelea's knife. Mitchell hauled him back onto his feet. Fegarty screamed in impotent rage.

"You did that, Mitchell. He killed Dominick just like he did Timothy, Margaret." Margaret Campbell's face was a ghastly portrait of horror and disbelief as it was caught in a shaft of moonlight silently invading the church. But Mitchell knew the danger had not reduced at all.

"Fegarty, you're a snivelling liar. Was this what you really wanted, Mrs Campbell? A re-run of that happening at the wall that day? A re-run of the bloody and brutal horror of a day when the men who did make it over the wall met their deaths immediately their boots touched the ground? Bayoneted half-a-dozen times by a crouching enemy on the other side? And who was to know they were waiting there? Not a single person, not me, not Alan Sinclair. We escaped Tim's fate by being caught up in that explosion, blown off the wall, the wall Eliza was crouching against." Margaret Campbell roused herself from the shock she was in and looked Mitchell straight in the eye.

"You and Alan Sinclair ordered Timothy to go over it," she suddenly screamed.

"He was a soldier. We all were. It was our duty. Duty! You should understand that, Mrs Campbell."

"Lady Grant saw the report submitted by Sir Ian. It stated that Alan Sinclair and then you had issued the orders. Timothy was only a private soldier, you were his corporal that day. Timothy was a good man, he was a brave one."

"He was a deserter, like his lying cousins. He abandoned his comrades when they faced possible death," said Mitchell ruthlessly. Margaret Campbell shook her head vigorously.

"No! Michael and Dominick deserted after that battle because of what had happened to Timothy."

"Who told you that, Mrs Campbell? Those two liars egged on by Lady Grant? I helped bury two unrecognisable bodies earlier that day with Fegarty's and Killelea's possessions on them. That's how they were identified. All too pat. I had already served with them, knew them for the kind of scum they were. There was no way they could have been with Tim on that wall for they had already deserted."

"Shut up, Mitchell. You're the liar here." Mitchell ignored Fegarty. Margaret Campbell now could not contain her anger and bitterness

"You forced Timothy over. Lady Grant told me." She had only been half-listening. Mitchell had to make her understand.

"You and Killelea were not at that action, Fegarty. None of you had any intentions of being there. Joe Petherbridge was on and off that hill long before the action took place. Dominick knew that bit of information and told the monks it at breakfast. You two could only have known about his presence there if you had met him. So, you were the ones who had tried to get into the Naval Brigade's boat earlier that day. That was the real reason Dominick hated the marines. Nothing really to do with Timothy at all. Timothy had gone back up to his regiment for there was no where else to go and he performed as the soldier he was. Michael, was trying to kill Petherbridge a little side event just for the two of you? Did you know about Joe Petherbridge, Mrs Campbell? I thought not." Margaret Campbell suddenly plucked the bayonet from Killelea's dead hand, the blood dripping from it unnoticed. Fegarty sensed the danger he was now in and lunged but she was too quick for him and the lethal blade sliced through the air, inches from his thick sleeve. He backed off, tripped clumsily over the stomach-churning

126

remains of his cousin and broke into a run. The darkness echoed to the rushing clatter of their footsteps until all was silent for a while but for the scraping sound of a bench on the floor of the Lady Chapel as Jude sat down heavily upon it, his head resting in his clammy hands.

"It's alright, son," said Mitchell quietly, his hand resting for a moment on the boy's shivering shoulder. "It's all over." Jude dragged himself to his feet and went in search of a piscina. He plunged his head into the first one he came to and its holy water did the trick in a very non-religious kind of way. A cold, bitterly cold, wake-up call.

Margaret Campbell stood a short distance from Fegarty's body as it lay sprawled in the Lady Chapel and gazed intently at it. His own knife had skewered him. A sliding trail of blood bore witness to the skidding path he had taken as he had slipped on his cousin's gore.

"He probably picked the mess up on his boots when he stumbled over Killelea's body in the aisle." Mitchell did not know why he had bothered to explain that.

"Had it really been all her idea? Lady Grant's?" Margaret Campbell spoke quietly, very controlled.

"Yes. Simple jealousy and pride. She knew about Lucy. She urged Killelea and Fegarty on. They were scum but with enough decency to be riddled with guilt for leaving Timothy behind that day. They had quickly put their on papers onto two dead bodies. Timothy seems to have been too innocent a lad to even think of it. She probably even provided the money that was supposed to come from them for that's where the house and all the rest was supposed to have come from, wasn't it?" asked Mitchell. Mrs Campbell nodded. That was the only way, Mitchell guessed, she could have afforded that lifestyle.

"They said it was money that had come to me as Timothy's wife from selling some family farm-land in County Mayo."

"Margaret!" Eliza Cowan's voice echoed suddenly as she entered from the cloisters. "Come on. Lucy's asking for you." She walked slowly towards them, her eyes never leaving her sister. How much had she heard? Everything probably. Margaret Campbell glanced at her then her eyes went back once more to Fegarty. Eliza Cowan was quick to spot it.

"Don't Margaret."

"They didn't kill Tim but they killed me. All those years, all that hatred."

"No!" Eliza cried out as Margaret held the bayonet high above her head and Mitchell felt himself wince inside at the destruction she was about to wreak on Fegarty's dead body. It began its plunging descent and Mitchell spun Eliza away from the sight. But she wrenched herself free from his grasp and turned back to her sister as the sickening thud roared out. The bayonet quivered for a moment or two and then stood tall and straight, plunged up to the hilt in Lady Grant's coffin.

"I loved him so much, Eliza. I still love him." Margaret Campbell's voice was scarcely audible.

"I know." Eliza Cowan's arms were wrapped around her sister.

"They just used me. They were amused by my stupidity all those years. I don't really mind that for Duncan Mitchell was right, they were scum, all three of them, and it seems I was no better."

"Now, Mrs Campbell," Mitchell began and was quickly interrupted by her.

"A problem for you to solve, Mr Mitchell. When the bitterness has gone, what do you put in its place? If it's eaten up all the good feelings and thoughts, what do you have left?"

"Precisely nothing, Mrs Campbell." Margaret Campbell wanted only honesty after a lifetime of soul-destroying lies and Mitchell would not insult her with platitudes. "Well, not exactly nothing, for just asking that question means you still have the desire to replace what's gone with something better and that is most certainly a very positive beginning. You could regard it as a clean slate. The opportunity to start all over again from scratch. You're a Cowan woman, Mrs Campbell, and I've always found them pretty formidable." He was aware of Eliza Cowan staring at him in surprise. "Now, ladies, we are standing here knee-deep in corpses and I feel that young Jude over there and I ought to do something about it."

"Have the place sluiced out," Margaret Campbell suggested absently.

"Once a nurse, Mrs Campbell," said Mitchell approvingly. Eliza and Mitchell smiled in spite of everything. "I was actually thinking more along the lines of hauling Mr Fegarty over to join his cousin and then informing Father Prior. It's really quite a nice little nook this and Fegarty is definitely lowering the tone." But first he would remove the weapon from the coffin.

"Nothing new there," came a resentful voice. Mitchell tut-tutted.

"That is not a helpful or charitable comment , Brother Jude. It's as well you're leaving the religious life." Jude had wandered over but still assiduously avoided looking at Fegarty. "Now go and fetch a couple of sheets and then find Brother Walter. He is more practical where dead bodies are concerned than the Prior." Margaret Campbell began to leave. "I'll see you safely back to the guest-house, Mrs Campbell." Mitchell had suddenly begun to panic. He was afraid of what she might do to herself.

"No, please, I'd rather be on my own for a while."

"But you've had a great shock." Alarm bells were ringing in Mitchell's head and he glanced quickly at Eliza Cowan as her sister walked slowly out into the cloisters. "Goodnight, Mr Mitchell." Margaret Campbell's words seemed to echo forever in his head.

"Eliza! She's under enormous stress. What might she do?" Suicide, that was what his senses were screaming.

"Let her go, Mr Mitchell. Let her find her own kind of peace."

Chapter 12

Eliza Cowan stood by Mitchell's side in the all-embracing silence of the church as her sister slowly vanished from sight and Jude left to fetch Brother Walter.

"She'll be alright. I know her very well," she said at last trying to reassure him.

"She loved Timothy Campbell very much, didn't she?" Mitchell now felt very tired and was conscious once more of the throbbing in his head.

"Did she?" Eliza Cowan turned to face him and those ice-blue eyes bore into Mitchell's. He was deeply puzzled.

"Fifteen years of waiting, vowing to kill the people who she thought had harmed him. I'd call that a devoted kind of love." A ghost of a smile flitted across Eliza's pale, beautiful features as she slowly shook her head.

"My sister never really loved Timothy Campbell, Mr Mitchell. I thought you understood that. She has always been in love with Alan Sinclair. It was guilt that made her vow to avenge Timothy's death, not love. Margaret had gone to the Crimea to be near Alan. She'd told Timothy that the marriage was over a week before the Battle of Inkerman. She was sure that had played a part in his death, that he had ceased to care whether he lived or died. Major Sinclair has

131

never been aware of how she feels. To him, she's a friend, my sister, nothing more. The Cowans are not shackled by duty as you seem to think, Mr Mitchell, but by guilt." He stared at her and she shrugged. "Ironic, isn't it, Margaret and me? Family trait?" Mitchell stood looking silently at her, this latest revelation the final piece in the puzzle.

"Come away from here," he said at last, "come into Brother Conraitus's kitchen. It's the nearest thing to normality in this place." But she did not move. He walked over and removed the bayonet from its wooden grave. Mitchell turned to her as she spoke.

"Their son will mourn her and that's how it should be." She walked over and took her usual seat in front of the biers. He wondered what Alan Sinclair's reaction to it all would be. Unpredictable as always.

"Is that where you?" She faltered and looked towards the eastern aisle.

"That's where we'll lay them out, Jude and I, until the brothers take them to the charnel house." He stood judiciously between her and the sight of Fegarty's body.

"Dead at last," said Eliza Cowan softly, "and the wall got them, too, in the end. It was the will that finally made Lady Grant move after fifteen years of letting her hatred grow. For Margaret it was a terrible beauty right enough, her love for Alan. For Fegarty and Killelea and Lady Grant it must have been the longest-running laugh of their lives." She searched for her handkerchief and found it.

"They're not laughing now, none of them." Mitchell's face was grim as he spoke.

"I can't remember when I last really laughed either, Mr Mitchell. I don't think I'll ever laugh again."

"I could make you," he offered. She smiled broadly but did not laugh. He gave up.

"Lucy will make you laugh some day," he added quietly.

"I hope so," said Eliza Cowan, " but I hope more it will be the other way round." He handed her the envelope with the Christmas card in it that Captain Brogan had given him. She looked long and hard at the card and then gave him it back. "A prettier reminder of Christmas at Collinge Woods Priory. A new beginning for all of us. Pity it took all those deaths, though - two natural causes, two very nasty accidents and one murder to free us all." Mitchell followed her gaze as it rested upon Lady Grant's coffin. There were now no secrets between Eliza Cowan and Duncan Mitchell.

If you have enjoyed reading *The Ranks of Death* please leave a review on Amazon. Marie Rowan welcomes any constructive feedback.

Other books by Marie Rowan published by Moira Brown:

Mitchell Memoranda Series

Gorbals Chronicles Series

Dom Broadley Series (Young Adult)

27699843R00079

Printed in Great Britain
by Amazon